Also by George MacDonald Fraser

Flashman (1969)
Royal Flash (1970)
Flash for Freedom! (1972)
The Steel Bonnets (1972)
The General Danced at Dawn (1973)
Flashman at the Charge (1973)

McAuslan in the rough

George MacDonald Fraser, 1925-

McAuslan in the rough

and other stories

Alfred A. Knopf
New York
1974

THIS IS A BORZOI BOOK
PUBLISHED BY ALFRED A. KNOPF, INC.

Library of Congress Catalogue Card Number: 74–7720

ISBN: 0–394–49303–6

MANUFACTURED IN THE UNITED STATES OF AMERICA
FIRST AMERICAN EDITION

for Sie, Caro, and Nicky
some more stories

Contents

Author's note   viii

Glossary   x

Bo Geesty   3

Johnnie Cope in the morning   29

General knowledge, private information   51

Parfit gentil knight, but   87

Fly men   113

McAuslan in the rough   143

His Majesty says good-day   175

Author's note

When the first stories about Private McAuslan and Lieutenant Dand MacNeill were published four years ago, under the title *The General Danced at Dawn*, I prefaced them with the following foreword:

> The Highland battalion in this book never existed, inasmuch as the people in the stories are fictitious (with the formidable exception of my grandmothers), and the incidents have been made up from a wide variety of sources, including my imagination. As to traditions, customs, and one or two pieces of history, these too are a mixture, with one regimental strain predominating. But the atmosphere and background detail which I have tried to put into the book are as accurate as memory can make them.

That still holds good for the present book—despite the fact that various former Highland soldiers have been in touch with me, identifying characters and incidents in *The General Danced at Dawn*, sometimes even accurately. But since others, who have no connection with Scotland or its regiments, have written to tell me that the stories mirrored their own experiences in various armies and countries, I have come to the comforting conclusion that MacNeill and McAuslan are probably universal.

But one thing obviously is not, and that is the vocabulary of the Scottish soldier. It has been suggested (most forcibly from the United States) that I should have included a glossary and pronunciation guide to help the uninitiated through the mysteries of the Glasgow dialect. This presents difficulties, since some Glasgow expressions are virtually untranslatable, and mean very different things in different contexts. For example, the phrase "rerr terr" (literally, in English, "rare tear") can mean a good joke, or a happy occasion, or an exciting occurrence, or even a satisfactory fight. And, of course, language changes; the soldiers I write about are men of almost thirty years ago, and much of their slang is well out of date now.

Glasgow pronunciation I have tried to indicate in the spelling—which is only partly satisfactory. The simple word "pay" for instance, I have rendered "pey", because that is the nearest that spelling can come to the real pronunciation, which is something like the first vowel of the word "piper". But no written word can adequately convey the splendour of the Clydeside glottal stop, or reflect the whole state of mind embodied in the Glaswegian's habit of ending occasional sentences with the word "but", or in his emphatic prelude to any personal explanation—"See me?"

And they were not all Glaswegians—Aberdeenshire and the almost accentless Highland voices were frequently raised as well.

So with some trepidation, and defiant apologies in advance to those who may (and, knowing my fellow-countrymen, undoubtedly will) question the accuracy of my translation, I attach a short glossary not only of Scottish expressions but of British Army terms of the time.

G.M.F.

Glossary

banjo	to assault, beat up
bauchle	(v.) to shamble, to make a mess of; (n.) an awkward person
baur	a joke, a story (and, occasionally, a "rerr terr")
Billy Boys	a Glasgow gang of the period
brammer	a beauty, esp. of a girl. "Stotter" is synonymous
claim	to accost for the purpose of assault
cromach	long shepherd's crook carried by Highland colonels
glaur	mud, filth
greeting	weeping
humph	to heave, carry
keelie	a native Glaswegian; slightly derogatory when compared with London "cockney", Liverpool "scouse" or Newcastle "geordie"
manky	dirty
melt	to beat up
Naafi	canteen (Navy, Army and Air Force Institute)
namanahee	just so; that's it (Swahili)
O-group	Order group, at which commander outlines operations
oxter	armpit
Paurly Road	Parliamentary Road, in Glasgow
peching	panting, breathless
pit the heid on	lit. put the head on, i.e., to butt in the face
See's	lit. "see us", i.e., "give me"
sclim	to climb
shachle	to walk ungainly
shilpit	undersized, weakly
wog	an Egyptian, but loosely any native, esp. an Arab
yahoo	a barbarian (see Dean Swift)

McAuslan
in the
rough

Bo Geesty

See this fella, Bo Geesty? Aye, weel, him an' his
mates, they wis inna Foreign Legion, inna fort,
inna desert, an' the wogs wis gettin' tore in at them.
An' a' the fellas inna fort got killt, but when the
relief colyum arrived a' the fellas inna fort wis
staundin' up at the wall, wi' their guns an' bunnets
on, like they wis on guard. But they wis a' deid.
The fellas in the relief colyum couldnae make it
oot; they thought the place must be hauntit. So
they did. It wis a smashin' picture, but.
— Private McAuslan, as critic, on the film
of P. C. Wren's *Beau Geste*

Fort Yarhuna lies away to the south, on the edge of the
big desert. It was there, or something like it, in the days
when the Sahara was still grassland; in more modern
times it saw long-range patrols of Alexander the Great's
mercenaries from fair Cyrene across the sandhills eastward, and it received the battered remnants of Hannibal's regiments after Zama. It was garrisoned by Roman
legionaries before the Vandals swept into it from the
west, or Arab riders from the Great Sand Sea brought
the first camels and planted the date-palms in the little
village beneath its walls; it shielded the Barbary rovers'

sea-nests until a little detachment of U.S. Marines
marched across the desert to plant the Stars and Stripes
for the first time on foreign soil. The Caliphs ornamented
its gateway, the Crusaders built the little shrine in the
courtyard, the Afrika Korps stored the petrol for their
panzers in its stables, the Highland Division left their
inevitable "H.D." trademark on its walls, and Private
Fletcher (I suspect) scribbled "Kilroy was here" and
"Up the Celtic" on its main gate. That was during the
Twelve Platoon occupation, circa A.D. 1946.

The reason for Fort Yarhuna's long existence is that
it commands a crossing of the great caravan trails, the
last oasis on the edge of nowhere. The great trains from
the south, with their ivory and gold and slaves, paused
here before the last lap north to Tripoli and Tunis, or
before they turned eastward for Egypt; coming in the
other direction, it was where the Mediterranean traders
tightened their girths and sharpened their weapons
against the Touareg bandits who infested the southern
roads through the biggest wasteland in the world. Fort
Yarhuna, in fact, has seen a lot of hard service and is a
very hot station. Its importance to me is that it was my
first very own independent command, and the signifi-
cance of that is something which Hannibal's men, and
Alexander's, to say nothing of the Romans, Vandals,
Crusaders and Leathernecks, would be the first to
appreciate.

Why we had to garrison it, nobody knew. The battalion was stationed on the coast, in civilisation, the war
was over, and there was nothing to do except show the
flag, bathe, beat retreat every Friday with the pipes and
drums to impress the locals, and wait to be demobilised.
But Higher Authority, in Cairo, decreed that Fort
Yarhuna must be garrisoned—they may have had some
vague fears of invasion from the Belgian Congo, or been

unduly impressed by seeing *The Desert Song*, but more probably it was just military tidiness: Fort Yarhuna had always been manned, and it was officially in our battalion area. So, since I had been commissioned for six months and attained the giddy height of lieutenant, I was instructed to repair to Fort Yarhuna with two platoons, place it in a state of defence, occupy it for a month in the name of the King and the United Nations, close its gate at sunset, see that the courtyard was swept and free from litter, and in the event of an Arab uprising (I'm sure someone had seen *The Desert Song*) defend it to the last round and the last man etc., etc.

Of course, there wasn't a chance in a million of an Arab uprising. Since the Italians had been heaved out in the war, all that the genial Bedouin wanted to do was carry on loafing in the sun, catching cholera and plodding his caravans through Yarhuna village from nowhere to yonder; the nearest thing to illegal activity was the local pastime of looting the debris of war which Montgomery's and Rommel's men had left spread over the countryside, for in those days the whole way from Egypt to Tunis was a great junkyard of burned-out tanks, wrecked trucks, abandoned gear, and lost ammunition dumps. And whatever Cairo thought, the local official opinion was that the Arabs could have it, and welcome.

I was more concerned at the possibility of a Twelve Platoon uprising. A month stuck in a desert fort would be no joy to them, after the fleshpots of the coast, and while six months had established a pretty good working relationship between me and my volatile command of Glaswegians and Aberdeenshire countrymen, I was a trifle apprehensive of being their sole authority and mentor so far away from the battalion, where you have the whole apparatus of Army, Colonel, Regimental

Sergeant-Major and provost sergeant to back you up.

The Colonel, that kindly, crafty old gentleman, gave me sound advice before I set out. "Work 'em stupid," he said. "Every parade—reveille, first inspection, cook-house, and company office—must be on the dot, just as though you were in the battalion. Anyone drags his feet by as much as a second—nail him. I don't care if half the detachment's on jankers. But if you let 'em slack off, or have time to be bored, they'll be sand-happy before you know it. It can happen well inside a month; ennui has undermined more outpost garrisons than plague or enemy action, take my word for it." And he went on to tell me harrowing tales of Khyber forts and East African jungle stockades, called for another whisky, and assured me it would be great fun, really.

"To keep you occupied, you're to dig for water, *inside* the fort itself. The place hasn't been occupied for years, but there's got to be a well somewhere, the Sappers say. If one is found, it'll save the water-truck coming down every second day. You can pick up the drilling equipment at Marble Arch depot—they'll give you a driver to work it—while Keith takes the detachment down to Fort Yarhuna and settles 'em in."

Keith was the second-lieutenant who commanded Eleven Platoon—the garrison of Yarhuna was to be a two-platoon force—so I despatched him and the command to the fort, while I went with one section to Marble Arch for the drilling gear. It was a long, dusty, two-day haul east on the coast road, but we collected the drilling-truck from the Service Corps people, were shown how the special screw attached to its rear axle could drill a ten-foot shaft six inches across in a matter of minutes, and told that all we had to do was proceed by trial and error until we struck water.

I was in haste to get back along the coast and down to Fort Yarhuna to assume command before Keith did anything rash—young subalterns are as jealous as prima donnas, and convinced of each others' fecklessness, and Keith was a mere pink-cheeked one-pipper of twenty years, whereas I had reached the grizzled maturity of twenty-one and my second star. Heaven knew what youthful folly he might commit without my riper judgement to steady him. However, we paused for a brief sight-see at Marble Arch which, as you may know, is one of the architectural curiosities of North Africa, being a massive white gateway towering some hundreds of feet out of the naked desert, a grandiose tombstone to Mussolini's vanity and brief empire.

It was probably a mistake to stop and look at it: I should have remembered that in the section with me was Private McAuslan, the dirtiest soldier in the world, of whom I have written elsewhere. Short, be-pimpled, permanently unwashed, and slow-witted to a degree in the performance of his military duties, he was a kind of battalion landmark, like the Waterloo snuff-box. Not that he was a bad sort, in his leprous way, but he was sure disaster in any enterprise to which he set his grimy hand. As his platoon commander, I had mixed feelings about him, partly protective but mostly despairing. What made it worse was that he tried to please, which could lead to all sorts of embarrassment.

When we got out of the truck to view the arch he stood scratching himself and goggling balefully up at it, inquiring of his friend Private Fletcher:

"Whit the hell's yon thing?"

"Yon's the Marble Arch, dozey."

"Ah thought the Marble Arch wis in London. Sure it is."

"This is anither Marble Arch, ye dope."

"Aw." Pause. "Who the hell pit it here, then? Whit fur?"

"The Eyeties did. Mussolini pit it up, just for the look o' the thing."

McAuslan digested this, wiped his grimy nose, and like the Oriental sage meditating on human vanity, observed: "Stupid big bastard", which in its own way is a fair echo of contemporary opinion of Il Duce as an imperialist.

The trouble was that they wanted to climb the thing, and I was soft enough to let them; mind you, I wanted to climb it myself. And Marble Arch is really big; you climb it by going into a tiny door in one of its twin columns, ascending some steps, and then setting off, in total darkness, up an endless series of iron rungs driven into the wall. They go up forever, with only occasional rests on solid ledges which you find by touch in the gloom, and when you have climbed for about ten minutes, and the tiny square of light at the top of the shaft seems as small as ever, and your muscles are creaking with the strain of clinging to the rungs, you suddenly realise that the black abyss below you is very deep indeed, and if you let go. . . . Quite.

McAuslan, naturally, got lost. He strayed on to one of the ledges, apparently found another set of rungs somewhere, and roamed about in the stygian void, blaspheming horribly. His rich Parkhead oaths boomed through the echoing tunnels like the thunderings of some fearful Northern god with a glottal stop, and the ribaldries of the rest of the section, all strung out in the darkness on that frightening ladder, mocking him, turned the shaft into a deafening Tower of Babel. I was near the top, clinging with sweating fingers to the rungs, painfully aware that I couldn't go back to look for him —it would have been suicide to try to get past the other climbers in the blackness—and that if he missed his hold, or got exhausted playing Tarzan, we would finish up scraping him off the distant floor with a spoon.

"Don't panic, McAuslan," I called down. "Take it easy and Sergeant Telfer'll get you out." Telfer was at the tail of the climbing procession, I knew, and could be depended on.

'Ah'm no' —— panickin'" came the despairing wail from the depths. "Ah'm loast! Ach, the hell wi' this! —— Mussolini, big Eyetie git! Him an' his bluidy statues!" And more of the like, until Telfer found him, crouched on a ledge like a disgruntled Heidelberg man, and drove him with oaths to the top.

Once at the summit, you are on a platform between two enormous gladiatorial figures which recline along the top of the arch, supporting a vast marble slab which is the very peak of the monument. You get on to it by climbing a short iron ladder which goes through a hole in the slab, and there you are, with the wind howling past, looking down over the unfenced edge at the tiny toy trucks like beetles on the desert floor, a giddy drop below, and the huge sweep of sand stretching away to the hazy horizon, with the coast road like a string running dead straight away both sides of the arch. You must be able to see the Mediterranean as well, but curiously enough I don't remember it, just the appalling vastness of desert far beneath, and the forced cheerfulness of men pretending they are enjoying the view, and secretly wishing they were safely back at ground level.

We probably stayed longer than we wanted, keeping back from the edge or approaching it on our stomachs, because the prospect of descent was not attractive. Eventually I went first, pausing on the lower platform to instruct McAuslan to stay close above me, but not, as he valued his life, to tread on my fingers. He nodded,

ape-like, and then, being McAuslan, and of an inquiring
mind, asked me how the hell they had got they dirty big
naked statues a' the way up here, sir. I said I hadn't the
least idea, Fletcher said: "Sky-hooks", and as we groped
our way down that long, gloomy shaft, clinging like
flies, a learned debate was being conducted by the unseen climbers descending above me, McAuslan informing Fletcher that he wisnae gaunae be kidded and if
Fletcher knew how they got they dirty big naked statues
up there, let him say so, an' no' take the mickey oot o'
him, McAuslan, because he wisnae havin' it, see? We
reached the bottom, exhausted and shaking slightly, and
resumed our journey to Fort Yarhuna, myself digesting
another Lesson for Young Officers, namely: don't let
your men climb monuments, and if they do, leave
McAuslan behind. Mind you, leaving McAuslan behind
is a maxim that may be applied to virtually any situation.

We reached Yarhuna after another two-day ride,
branching off the coast road and spending the last eight
hours bumping over a desert track which got steadily
worse before we rolled through Yarhuna village and up
to the fort which stands on a slight rise quarter of a mile
farther on.

One look at it was enough to transport you back to
the Saturday afternoon cinemas of childhood, with
Ronald Colman tilting his kepi rakishly, Brian Donlevy
shouting "March or die, mes enfants", and the Riffs
coming howling over the sand-crests singing "Ho!" It
was a dun-coloured, sand-blasted square structure of
twenty-foot walls, with firing-slits on its parapet and a
large tower at one corner, from which hung the D
Company colour, wherever Keith had got that from.
Inside the fort proper there was a good open parade
square, with barracks and offices all round the inside of

the walls, their flat roofs forming a catwalk from which the parapet could be manned. It was your real Beau Geste fort, and it was while my section was debussing that I heard McAuslan recalling his visit to the pictures to see Gary Cooper in Wren's classic adventure story. ("Jist like Bo Geesty, innit, Wullie? Think the wogs'll get tore in at us, eh? Hey, mebbe Darkie'll prop up wir deid bodies like that bastard o' a sergeant in the pictur'." I'll wear gloves if I prop you up, I thought.)

Keith, full of the pride of possession, showed me round. He had done a good job in short order: the long barrack-rooms were clean if airless, all the gear and furniture had been unloaded, the empty offices and store-rooms had been swept clear of the sand that forever blew itself into little piles in the corners, and he had the Jocks busy whitewashing the more weather-worn buildings. Already it looked like home, and I remember feeling that self-sufficient joy that is one of the phenomena of independent command; plainly Keith and the Jocks felt it, too, for they had worked as they'd never have done in the battalion. I went through every room and office, from the top of the tower to the old Roman stable and the cool, musty cells beneath the gate-house, prying and noting, whistling "Blue heaven and you and I", and feeling a growing pleasure that this place was ours, to keep and garrison and, if necessary, defend. It was all very romantic, and yet practical and worthwhile—you can get slightly power-crazy in that sort of situation, probably out of some atavistic sense inherited from our ancestors, feeling secure and walled-in against the outside. It's a queer feeling, and I knew just enough from my service farther east to be aware that in a day or two it would change into boredom, and the answer, as the Colonel had said, was to keep busy.

So I was probably something like Captain Bligh in

the first couple of days, chasing and exhorting, keeping half the detachment on full parade within the fort itself, while the other half went out on ten-mile patrols of the area, for even with a friendly population in peacetime you can't know too much about the surrounding territory. To all intents it was just empty desert with a few Bedouin camps, apart from Yarhuna village itself. This was a fair-sized place, with its oasis and palm-grove, its market and some excellent Roman ruins, and about a hundred permanent huts and little houses. It boasted a sheikh, a most dignified old gentleman whose beard was bright red at the bottom and white near his mouth, where the dye had worn off; he visited us on our second day, and we received him formally, both platoons in their tartans and with fixed bayonets, presenting arms. He took it like a grandee, and Keith and I entertained him to tea in the company office, with tinned salmon sandwiches, club cheese biscuits, Naafi cakes, a tin of Players and such other delicacies as one lays before the face of kings. The detachment cook had had fits beforehand, because he wasn't sure if Moslems ate tinned salmon; as it turned out this one did, in quantity.

He had an interpreter, a smooth young man who translated into halting English the occasional observations of our guest, who sat immovable, smiling gently beneath his embroidered black kafilyeh, his brown burnous wrapped round him, as he gazed over the square at the Jocks playing football. We were staying for a month? And then? Another regiment would arrive? It was to be a permanent garrison, in fact? That would be most satisfactory; the British presence was entirely welcome, be they Tripoli Police or military. Yes, the local inhabitants had the happiest recollections of the Eighth Army—at this point the sheikh beamed and said the only word of English in his vocabulary,

which was "Monty!" with a great gleam of teeth. We
required nothing from the village? Quite so, we were
self-sufficient in the fort, but he would be happy to be of
assistance. . . . And so on, until after more civilities and
another massive round of salmon sandwiches, the sheikh
took a stately leave. It was at the gate that he paused,
and through his interpreter addressed a last question:
we were not going to alter or remove any of the fort
buildings during our stay? It was a very old place, of
course, and he understood the British valued such
things . . . a smile and a wave took in the carved gateway, and the little Crusaders' shrine (that surprised me,
slightly, I confess). We reassured him, he bowed, I
saluted, and the palaver was finished.

I'm not unduly fanciful, but it left me wondering just
a little. Possibly it's a legacy of centuries of empire, but
the British military are suspicious of practically everyone overseas, especially when they're polite. I summoned
the platoon sergeants, and enjoined strict caution in any
dealings we might have with the village. I'd done that
at the start, of course, parading the whole detachment
and warning them against (1) eating fruit from the
market, (2) becoming involved with local women, (3)
offending the dignity or religious susceptibilities of the
men, and (4) drinking native spirits. The result had been
half a dozen cases of mild dysentery; a frantic altercation between me, Private Fletcher (the platoon Casanova), and a hennaed harpy of doubtful repute; a brawl
between McAuslan and a camelman who had allegedly
stolen McAuslan's sporran; and a minor riot in Eleven
Platoon barrack-room which ended with the confisca-
tion of six bottles of arak that would have corroded a
stainless steel sink. All round, just about par for the
course, and easily dealt with by confinement to the fort
for the offenders.

That in itself was a sobering punishment, for Yarhuna village was an enchanting place apart from its dubious fleshpots. Every day or so a little caravan would come through, straight out of the Middle Ages, with its swathed drivers and jingling bells and veiled outriders each with his Lee Enfield cradled across his knee and his crossed cartridge belts. (What the wild men of the world will do when the last Lee Enfield wears out, I can't imagine; clumsy and old-fashioned it may be, but it will go on shooting straight when all the repeaters are rusty and forgotten.) The little market was an Arabian Nights delight with its interesting Orientals and hot cooking smells and laden stalls—lovely to look at, but hellish to taste—and I have an affectionate memory of a party of Jocks, bonnets pulled down, standing silently by the oasis tank, watching the camels watering, while the drivers and riders regarded the Jocks in turn, both sides quietly observing and noting, and reflecting on the quaint appearance of the foreigners. And for one day a travelling party of what I believe were Touaregs camped beyond the village, a cluster of red tents and cooking fires, and hooded men in black burnouses, with the famous indigo veils tight across their faces and the long swords at their girdles. They made no attempt to speak to us, but a few of them rode up to watch Twelve Platoon drilling outside the gate; they just sat their camels, immovable, until the parade was over, and then turned and rode off.

"There's your real Arabis," said Sergeant Telfer, and without my telling him he posted four extra sentries that night, one to each wall. He reported what he had done, almost apologetically; like me, he felt that we were playing at Foreign Legionnaires, rather, but still. . . . Everything was quiet, the natives were friendly, the platoons were hard-worked and happy, and it was a

good time to take precautions. We were in the second
week of our stay, and there was just the tiniest sense of
unease creeping into everyone's mind. Perhaps it was
boredom, or the fact of being cooped up every night in
a stronghold—for what? Perhaps it was the desert, hot
as a furnace floor during the day, a mystery of silver and
shadow and silence by night; as you stood on the parapet and looked out across the empty dunes, you felt very
small indeed and helpless, for you were in the presence
of something that had seen it all, through countless ages,
something huge beside which you were no bigger than
an ant. It was a relief to come down the steps to my
quarters, and hear the raucous Glasgow patter from the
cheerful barrack-room across the square.

And still nothing happened—why should it, after all?
—until the beginning of the third week, when we
started drilling for water. We had lost the first two
weeks because of some defective part in the rear-axle
drilling mechanism, and a spare had taken time to
obtain from Marble Arch. It was a minor inconvenience,
for the water-truck came from the coast three times a
week, but a well would be a good investment for the
future, for the only alternative water-supply was the
oasis, and one look at its tank, with camels slurping,
infants paddling, horses fertilising, grandmothers washing the family's smalls, and everyone disposing prodigally
of their refuse, suggested that our little blue and yellow
purification pills would have had an uphill fight.

With the truck fixed, we looked for a likely spot to
drill.

"We need a diviner," I said. "One of those chaps with
a hazel stick who twitches."

"How about McAuslan?" suggested Keith. "He's
allergic to water; all we have to do is march him up and
down till he starts shuddering, and that's the spot."

Eventually we decided just to drill at random, in various parts of the parade ground, for none of the buildings contained anything that looked remotely like the remains of a well. I tried to remember what I had ever learned of medieval castle or Roman camp lay-out —for Yarhuna's foundations were undoubtedly Roman— prayed that we wouldn't disturb any temples of Mithras or Carthaginian relics, and went to it. We drilled in several parts of the square, and hit nothing but fine dry sand and living rock. Not a trace of water. Some of the locals had loafed up to the gate to watch our operations, but they had no helpful suggestions to offer, so at retreat we closed the gates, put away the drilling-truck, and decided to have another shot next day.

And that night, for the first time, the ghost of Fort Yarhuna walked.

That, at least, was the conclusion reached by Private McAuslan, student of the occult and authority on lonely desert outposts, whose Hollywood-fed imagination could find no other explanation when the facts reached his unwashed ears, as they did next morning. What had happened was this.

On the cold watch, the one from 2 to 4 a.m., the sentry on the parapet near the tower had seen, or thought he had seen, a shadowy figure under the tower wall, just along from his sentry beat. He had challenged, received no reply, and on investigating had found— nothing. Puzzled, but putting it down to his imagination, he had resumed his watch, and just before 4 a.m. he had *felt*—he emphasised the word—someone watching him from the same place. He had turned slowly, and caught a fleeting glimpse of a form, no more, but again the parapet had been empty when he went to look. He raised no alarm at the time, because, with Highland logic, he had decided that since there was nothing there,

there was nothing to raise an alarm for, but he had told Sergeant Telfer in the morning, and Telfer told me.

I saw him in my office, a tall, fair, steady lad from the Isles, called Macleod. "You didn't get a good clear sight of anyone?" I said.

"No, sir."

"Didn't hear anyone drop from the parapet, either into the fort or over the wall into the desert?"

"No, sir."

"No marks to show anyone had been there?"

"No, sir."

"Nothing missing or been disturbed, Sergeant Telfer?"

"Nothing, sir."

"Well, then," I said to Macleod, "it looks like the four o'clock jump—we all know what can happen on stag; you think you see things that aren't there . . ."

"Yes, sir," said Macleod, "I've had that. I wouldnae swear I *saw* anything at all, sir." He paused. "But I felt something."

"You mean something touched you?"

"Nat-at-at, sir. I mean I chust *felt* some-wan thair. Oh, he wass thair, right enough."

It was sweating hot in the office, but I suddenly felt a shiver on my spine, just in the way he said it, because I knew exactly what he meant. Everyone has a sixth sense, to some degree, and most of its warnings are purely imaginary, but when a Highlander, and a Skye man at that, tells you, in a completely matter-of-fact tone, that he has "felt" something, you do not, if you have any sense, dismiss or scoff at it as hallucination. Macleod was a good soldier, and not a nervous or sensational person; he meant exactly what he said.

"A real person—a man?" I said, and he shook his head.

"I couldnae say, sir. It wasnae wan of our laads, though; I'm sure about that."

I didn't ask him why he was sure; he couldn't have told me.

"Well, he doesn't seem to have done any damage, whoever he was," I said, and dismissed him. I asked Telfer, who was a crusty, tough Glaswegian with as much spiritual sensitivity as a Clyde boiler, what he thought, and he shrugged.

"Seein' things," he said. "He's a good lad, but he's been starin' at too much sand."

Which was my own opinion; I'd stood guard often enough to know what tricks the senses could play. But Macleod must have mentioned his experience among his mates, for during the morning, while I was supervising the water-drilling, there came Private Watt to say that he, too, had things to report from the previous night. While on guard above the main gate, round about midnight, he had heard odd sounds at the foot of the wall, outside the fort, and had leaned out through an embrasure, but seen nothing. (Why, as he spoke, did I remember that P.C. Wren story about a sentry in a desert fort leaning out as Watt had done, and being snared by a bolas flung by hostile hands beneath?) But Watt believed it must have been a pi-dog from the village; he wouldn't have mentioned it, but he had heard about Macleod. . .

I dismissed the thing publicly, but privately I couldn't help wondering. Watt's odd noises were nothing in themselves, but considered alongside Macleod's experience they might add up to—what? One noise, one sand-happy sentry—but sand-happy after only two weeks? And yet Fort Yarhuna was a queer place; it had got to me, a little, in a mysterious way—but then I knew I was devilled with too much imagination, and being the man

in charge I was probably slightly jumpier with responsibility than anyone else.

I pushed it aside, uneasily, and could have kicked the
idiot who must have mentioned the word "ghost" some
time that day. That was the word that caught the primitive thought-process of McAuslan, and led him to
speculate morbidly on the fate of the graveyard garrison
of Fort Zinderneuf, which had held him spellbound in
the camp cinema.

"It'll be yin o' they fellas frae Bo Geesty," he informed
an admiring barrack-room. "He's deid, but he cannae
stay aff parade. Clump-clump, up an' doon the stair a'
night, wi' a bullet-hole in the middle o' his heid. Ah'm
tellin' ye. Hey, Macleod, did your bogle hiv a hole in his
heid?"

"You'll have wan in yours, McAuslan, if ye don't shut
upp," Macleod informed him pleasantly. "No' that mich
will come oot of it, apart from gaass."

My batman, who told me about this exchange, added
that the fellas had egged McAuslan on until he, perceiv-
ing himself mocked, had gone into sulky silence, warning
them that the fate of Bo Geesty would overtake them,
an' then they'd see. Aye.

And thereafter it was forgotten about—until the
following morning, at about 5 a.m., when Private
McLachlan, on guard above the main gate, thought he
heard unauthorised movement somewhere down in the
parade square and, being a practical man, challenged,
and turned out the guard. There were two men fully
awake in the gate-guardroom, and one of them, hurry-
ing out in response to McLachlan's shout, distinctly saw
—or thought he distinctly saw—a shadowy figure disappearing into the gloom among the buildings across
the square.

"Bo Geesty!" was McAuslan's triumphant verdict, for

that side of the square contained the old stables, the
company office, and Keith's and my sleeping-quarters,
and not a trace of anyone else was to be found. And
Keith, who had been awake and reading, was positive
that no one had passed by following McLachlan's challenge ("Halt-who-goes-there! C'moot, ye b—— o' hell,
Ah see ye!")

It was baffling, and worrying, for no clue presented
itself. The obvious explanation was that we were being
burgled by some Bedouin expert from the oasis—but if
so, he was an uncommon good second-storeyman, who
could scale a twenty-foot wall and go back the same
way, unseen by sentries (except, possibly, by Macleod),
and who didn't steal anything, for the most thorough
check of stores and equipment revealed nothing missing. No, the burglar theory was out. So what remained?

A practical joker inside? Impossible; it just wasn't
their style. So we had the inescapable conclusion that it
was a coincidence, two men imagining things on successive nights. I chose that line, irascibly examined and
dismissed McLachlan and his associates with instructions *not* to hear or see mysterious figures unless they
could lay hands on them, held a square-bashing parade
of both platoons to remind everyone that this was a
military post and not Borley Rectory, put the crew of
the drilling-truck to work again on their quest for a
well, and retired to my office, a disquieted subaltern.
For as I had watched the water-drill biting into the sand
of the square, another thought struck me—a really
lunatic idea, which no one in his right mind would
entertain.

Everything had been quiet in Fort Yarhuna until we
started tearing great holes in the ground, and I remembered my hopes that we wouldn't disturb any historic
buried ruin or Mythraic temple or ancient tomb or—

anything. You see the train of thought—this was a fort
that had been here probably since the days when the
surrounding land had been the Garden of Eden—so the
Bedouin say, anyway—and ancient places have an aura
of their own, especially in the old desert. You don't
disturb them lightly. So many people had been through
this fort—Crusaders, barbarians, Romans, Saracens, and
so on, leaving something of themselves behind forever,
and if you desecrate such a place, who knows what
you'll release? Don't misunderstand me, I wasn't imagining that our drilling for water had released a spirit from
its tomb deep in the foundations—well, not exactly, not
in as many words that I'd have cared to address to anyone, like Keith, for example. That was ludicrous, as I
looked out of my office and watched the earthy soldiery
grunting and laughing as they refilled yet another dead
hole and the truck moved on to try again. The sentry on
the gate, Telfer's voice raised in thunderous rebuke,
someone singing in the cookhouse—this was a real,
military world, and ghosts were just nonsense. More
things in heaven and earth . . . *ex Africa semper aliquid
novi* . . . Private McAuslan's celluloid-inspired fancies
. . . a couple of tired sentries . . . my own Highland
susceptibility to the fey. . . . I snapped "Tach!" impatiently in the fashion of my MacDonald granny,
strode out of my office and showed Private Forbes how
to take penalty kicks at the goal which the football
enthusiasts had erected near the gate, missed four out of
six, and retired grinning amidst ironic cheers, feeling
much better.

But that evening, after supper, I found myself mounting the narrow stairway to the parapet where the sentries were just going on first stag. It was gloaming, and
the desert was taking on that beautiful star-lit sheen
under the purple African sky that is so incredibly lovely

that it is rather like a coloured postcard in bad taste. The fires and lights were twinkling away down in the village, the last fawn-orange fringe of daylight was dwindling beyond the sand-hills, the last warm wind was touching the parapet, the night stillness was falling on the fort and the shadowy dunes, and Private Brown was humming "Ye do the hokey-cokey and ye turn aroond" as he clattered up the stairway to take his post, rifle in hand. Four sentries, one to each wall—and only my imagination could turn the silhouette of a bonneted Highlander into a helmeted Roman leaning on his hasta, or a burnoused mercenary out of Carthage, or a straight-nosed Greek dreaming of the olive groves under Delphi, or a long-haired savage from the North wrapping his cloak about him against the night air. They had all been here, and they were all long gone—perhaps. And if you smile at the perhaps, wait until you have stood on the wall of a Sahara fort at sundown, watching the shadows lengthen and the silence creep across the sand invisible in the twilight. Then smile.

I went down at last, played beggar-my-neighbour with Keith for half an hour, read an old copy of the *Tripoli Ghibli* for a little while longer, and then turned in. I didn't drop off easily; I heard the midnight stag change over, and then the two o'clock, and then I must have dozed, for the next thing I remember is waking suddenly, for no good reason, and lying there, lathered in sweat that soaked the clean towel which was our normal night attire, listening. It took a moment to identify it: a cautious scraping noise, as of a giant rat, somewhere outside. It wasn't any sound I knew, and I couldn't locate it, but one thing was certain, it hadn't any business to be going on.

I slid out and into my trousers and sandals, and stood listening. My door was open, and I went forward and listened again. There was no doubt of it; the sound was coming from the old stable, about twenty yards to my left, against the east wall. Irregular, but continuous, scrape-scrape. I glanced around; there were sentries visible in the dying moonlight on the catwalks to either side, and straight ahead on the gate-wall; plainly they were too far away to hear.

As silently as possible, but not furtively, for I didn't want the sentries to mistake me, I turned right and walked softly in front of the office, and then cut across the corner of the parade. The sentry on the catwalk overhead stiffened as he caught sight of me, but I waved to him and went on, towards the guardroom. I was sweating as I entered, and I didn't waste time.

"Get Sergeant Telfer, quietly. Tell him to come to the stable, not to make a sound. You three, come with me; you, McNab, up to the parapet, and tell the sentries on no account to fire until I give the word. Move."

Thank God, you don't have to tell Jocks much when there's soldiering to do; within five minutes that stable was boxed as tight as a drum—four of us in front of it, in line, crouching down; two riflemen some yards behind, to back up, and two men with torches ready to snap on. The scraping sound was still going on in the stable, quite distinctly, and I thought I could hear someone gasping with exertion. I nodded to Telfer, and he and one of the Jocks crept forward to the stable door, one to each of the heavy leaves; I could see Telfer's teeth, grinning, and then I snapped—"Now!", the doors were hauled back, the torches went on—and there they were.

Three Arabs, glaring into the torch-light, two of them with shovels, a half-dug hole in the floor—and then they came hurtling out, and I went for the knees of the nearest, and suddenly remembered trying to tackle Jack

Ramsay as he came weaving through our three-quarters at Old Anniesland, and how he'd dummied me. This wasn't Ramsay, though, praise God; he came down with a yelp and a crash, and one of the Jocks completed his ruin by pinning him by the shoulders. I came up, in time to see Telfer and another Jock with a struggling Arab between them, and the third one, who hadn't even got out of the stable, being submerged by a small knot of Highlanders, one of whom was triumphantly croaking "Bo Geesty!" No doubt of it, McAuslan had his uses when the panic was on.

We quieted the captives, after a moment or two, but there wasn't a word to be got out of them, and nothing to be deduced from their appearance except that they weren't genuine desert Buddoos, but more probably from the village or some place farther afield. Two of them were in shirts and trousers, and none of them was what you would call a stalwart savage; more like fellaheen, really. I consigned them to the guardroom, ordered a fifty per cent stand-to on the walls, and turned to examine the stable.

They had dug a shallow hole, no more, in the middle of the stable, and the reek was appalling. Camel stables are odorous at the best of times, and this one had been accommodating beasts, probably, since Scipio's day. But we had to see what they'd been after, and since a good officer shouldn't ask his men to do what he won't do himself . . . I was eyeing one of the fallen shovels reluctantly when a voice spoke at my elbow.

"Jings!" it said. "Hi, sir, mebbe it's treasure! Burried treasure!"

I wouldn't have thought McAuslan's deductive powers that fast, myself, but he explained that there had been treasure in Bo Geesty—"a jool, the Blue Watter, that Bo Geesty pinched aff his aunty, so he did." From the glittering light in his eye I could see that his powers of identification would shortly lead him to the dream-stage where he was marrying Susan Hayward, so I indicated the shovel and asked him would he like to test his theory.

He began digging like a demented Nibelung, choking only occasionally as his shovel released noxious airs, exclaiming "Aw, jeez!" before falling to again with energy. His comrades stood aside as he hurled great lumps of the ordure of centuries from the hole—even for McAuslan, I decided this was too much, and offered to have him spelled, but he wouldn't hear of it. He entertained us, in gasps as he dug, with a synopsis of the plot of *Beau Geste*, but I can't say I paid much attention, for I was getting excited. Whatever the Arabs had been after, it must be something precious—and then his shovel rang, just like the best pirate stories, on something metallic.

We had it out in another five minutes, and my mounting hopes of earth-shaking archaeological discovery died as the torches revealed a twentieth-century metal box for mortar bombs—not British, but patently modern. I sent the others out, in case it was full of live ammo., and gingerly prised back the clasps and raised the lid. It was packed to bursting with papers, wedged almost into a solid mass, because the tin had not been proof against its surroundings, and it was with some difficulty that I worked one loose—it was green, and faded, but it was undoubtedly a bank-note. And so were all the rest.

They were, according to the Tripoli police inspector who came to examine them next day, pre-war Italian notes, and totally worthless. Which was a pity, since their total face value was well over a hundred million lire; I know, because I was one of the suffering members of the court of inquiry which had to count them, rank, congealed and stinking as they were. As the officer who had found them, I was an obvious candidate for membership of that unhappy court, when we got back to the battalion; I, a Tripoli police lieutenant, a major from the Pay Corps, and a subaltern from the Green Howards, who said that if he caught some contagious disease from this job he was going to sue the War Office. We counted very conscientiously for above five minutes, and then started computing in lumps; the Pay Corps man objected, and we told him to go to hell. He protested that our default of duty would be detected by higher authority, and the Green Howard said that if higher authority was game enough to catch him out by counting this lot note by note, then higher authority was a better man than he was. We settled on a figure of 100,246,718 lire, of which we estimated that 75,413,311 were too defaced to be accepted as currency, supposing the pre-war Italian government were still around to support them.

For the rest, the court concluded that the money had been buried by unknown persons from Yarhuna village, after having possibly been looted from the Italian garrison who had occupied the fort early in the war. The money had lain untouched until water-drilling operations, conducted by Lieutenant D. MacNeill, had alarmed the villagers, who might have supposed that their treasure was being sought, they being unaware that it was now quite worthless. Hence their attempts to enter the fort nocturnally on at least three occasions to remove their hoard, on the last of which they had been detected and apprehended. It was difficult to see, the court added, that proceedings could justifiably be taken against the three captured Arabs, and their release was recommended. Just for spite we also consigned the notes themselves to the care of the provost marshal, who was the pompous ass who had convened the court in the first place, and signed the report solemnly.

"Serve him right," grunted the Green Howard. "Let him keep them, and press 'em between the leaves of his confidential reports. Or burn 'em, if he's got any sense. What, you're not taking one of them, are you?—don't be mad, you'll catch the plague."

"Souvenir," I said. "Don't worry, the man it's going to is plague-proof."

And when I handed it over, with a suggestion that it should be disinfected in a strong solution of carbolic, McAuslan was enraptured.

"Och, ta, sir," he said, "that's awfy decent of ye."

"Not a bit; you're welcome if you want it. You dug it up. But it's worthless, mind; it won't buy anything."

He looked shocked, as though I had suggested an indecency.

"Ah widnae spend it," he protested. "Ah'll tak' it hame, for a souvenir. Nice to have, like—ye know, tae mind us of bein' inna desert." He went slightly pink. "The fellas think Ah'm daft, but Ah liked bein' inna fort—like inna Foreign Legion, like Gairy Cooper."

"You've been in the desert before, though. You were in the 51st, weren't you—Alamein and so on?"

"Aye, so Ah wis." He sniffed thoughtfully, and rubbed his grimy nose. "But the fort wis different."

So it was, but I didn't quite share his happy memories. As a platoon commander, I was painfully aware that it was the place where Arabs had three times got past my sentries by night. One up to them, one down to us. I was slightly cheered up when—and this is fact, as reported in the local press—a week later, the warehouse where the provost marshal had deposited his noisome

cache was broken into by night, and the caseful of useless lire removed. There was much speculation where it
had gone.

I can guess. Those persistent desert gentlemen probably have it down in Yarhuna village to this day, and
being simple men in some things, if not in breaking and
entering, they doubtless still believe that it is a valuable
nest-egg for their community. I don't know who garrisons Fort Yarhuna now—the Libyans, I suppose—but
if there's one thing I'd bet on, it is that when the military
move out again, shadowy figures will move in under the
old carved gate by night, and put the loot back in a
nice safe place. And who is to question their judgement?
Fort Yarhuna will still be there a thousand years after
the strongest banks of Europe and America have passed
into ruins.

Johnny Cope
in the
morning

When I was a very young soldier, doing my recruit
training in a snowbound wartime camp in Durham,
there was a villainous orderly sergeant who used to get
us up in the mornings. He would sneak silently into our
hut at 5.30 a.m., where we were frowsting in our coarse
blankets against the bitter cold of the room, suddenly
snap on all the lights, and start beating the coal-bucket
with the poker. At the same time two of his minions
would rush from bunk to bunk screaming:

"Wake-eye! Wake-eye! I can see yer! Gerrup! Gerrup!
Gerrup!"

And the orderly sergeant, a creature devoid of pity
and any decent feeling, would continue his hellish
metallic hammering while he shouted:

"Getcher cold feet on the warm floor! Har-har!" and
sundry obscenities of his own invention. Then all three
would retire, rejoicing coarsely, leaving behind them
thirty-six recruits suffering from nervous prostration, to
say nothing of ringing in the ears.

But it certainly woke us up, and as I did my first early
morning fatigue, which consisted of dragging a six-foot
wooden table-top down to the ablutions and scrubbing
it with cold water, I used to contrast my own miserable

lot with that of his late majesty Louis XIV of France, whose attendants used a very different technique to dig him out of his scratcher. As I recalled, a valet in velvet-soled shoes used to creep into the royal bedchamber at a fairly civilised hour, softly draw back the curtains a little way, and then whisper: "It is my humble duty and profound honour to inform your majesty that it is eight-thirty of the clock." That, now, is the way to break the bad news, and afterwards the body of majesty was more or less lifted out of bed by a posse of princes of the blood who washed, fed, watered and dressed him in front of the fire. No wooden tables to scrub for young Louis.

And as I wrestled with my brush in the freezing water, barking my knuckles and turning blue all over, I used to have daydreams in which that fiend of an orderly sergeant was transported back in time to old Versailles, where he would clump into the Sun-King's bedroom in tackety boots at 5.30, guffawing obscenely, thrashing the fire-irons against the fender, and bawling:

"Levez-vous donc, Jean Crapaud! Wake-eye, wake-eye! Getcher froid pieds on the chaud terre! I can see yer, you frog-eating chancer! Har-har!"

While I concede that this kind of awakening could have done Louis XIV nothing but good, and possibly averted the French Revolution, the whole point of the daydream was that the orderly sergeant would un-doubtedly be flung into an oubliette in the Bastille for lèse majesté, there to rot with his red sash and copy of King's Regulations, while virtuous recruits in the twen-tieth century drowsed on until the late forenoon.

And while I stood mentally picturing this happy state of affairs, and sponging the icy water off the table-top with the flat of my hand, the sadistic brute would sneak into the ablutions and turn the cold hose on us, scream-ing:

"Two minnits to gerron rifle parade, you 'orrible shower! Har-har! Mooo-ve or I'll blitz yer!"

I wonder that we survived that recruit training, I really do.

You may suppose that that orderly sergeant's method of intimating reveille was as refined a piece of mental cruelty as even a military mind could devise, and I daresay if I hadn't later been commissioned into a Highland regiment I would agree. But in fact, there I discovered something worse, and it used to happen once a week, regularly on Friday mornings. In nightmares I can hear it still.

On the other six days of the week reveille was sounded in the conventional way at six, by a bugler on the distant square playing the famous "Charlie, Charlie, get out of bed". If you were a pampered brute of an officer, you used to turn over, mumbling happily, and at six-thirty your orderly would come in with a mug of tea, open the shutters, lay out your kit, and give you the news of the day while you drank, smoked, and coughed contentedly.

But on Fridays it was very different. Then the duty of sounding reveille devolved on the battalion's pipes and drums, who were bound to march round the entire barrack area, playing full blast. The trouble was, in a spirit of *schadenfreud* comparable with that of the Durham orderly sergeant's, they used to assemble in dead silence immediately outside the junior subalterns' quarters, inflate their beastly bags without so much as a warning sigh, poise their drum-sticks without the suspicion of a click, and then, at a signal from that god-forsaken demented little kelpie of a pipe-sergeant, burst thunderously into the squealing cacophony and ear-splitting drum rolls of "Hey, Johnnie Cope, are ye waukin' yet?"

Now, "Johnnie Cope" is one of the most magnificent

sounds ever to issue from musical instruments. It is the Highlanders' war clarion, the tune that is played before battle, the wild music that is supposed to quicken the blood of the mountain man and freeze the foe in his tracks. It commemorates the day two and a quarter centuries ago when the broadswords came whirling out of the mist at Prestonpans to fall on Major-General John Cope's redcoats and cut them to ribbons in something under five minutes. I once watched the Seaforths go in behind it against a Japanese-held village, and saw for the first time that phenomenon which you can't really appreciate until you have seen it—the unbelievable speed with which Highland troops can accelerate a slow, almost leisurely advance into an all-out charge. And I've heard it at military funerals, after "Lovat's Lament" or "Flowers of the Forest", and never failed to be moved by it. Well played, it is a savage, wonderful sound, unlike any other pipe march—this, probably, because it doesn't truly belong to the Army, but to the fighting tails of the old clansmen before the government had the sense to get them into uniforms.

But whatever it does, for the Jocks or to the enemy, at the proper time and occasion, its effect at 6 a.m. on a refined and highly-strung subaltern who is dreaming of Rita Hayworth is devastating. The first time I got it, full blast at a range of six feet or so, through a thin shutter, with twenty pipers tearing their lungs out and a dozen side-drums crashing into the thunderous rhythm, I came out of bed like a galvanised ferret, blankets and all, under the impression that the Jocks had Risen, or that the MacLeods were coming to settle things with me and my kinsfolk at long last. My room-mate, a cultured youth of nervous disposition, shot bolt upright from his pillow with a wordless scream, and sat gibbering that the Yanks had dropped the Bomb, and, as usual, in the wrong place. For a few deafening moments we just absorbed it, with the furniture shuddering and the whole room in apparent danger of collapse, and then I flung open the shutters and rebuked the musicians, who were counter-marching outside.

Well, you try arguing with a pipe-band some time, and see what it gets you. And you cannot, if you are a young officer with any notions of dignity, hie yourself out in pyjamas and bandy words with a towering drum-major, and him resplendent in leopard skin and white spats, at that hour in the morning. So we had to endure it, while they regaled us with "The White Cockade" and the "Braes of Mar", before marching off to the strains of "Highland Laddie", and my room-mate said it had done something to his inner ear, and he doubted if he would ever be able to stand on one leg or ride a bicycle again.

"They can't do that to us!" he bleated, holding his nose and blowing out his cheeks in an effort to restore his shattered ear-drums. "We're officers, dammit!"

That, as I explained to him, was the point. Plainly what we had just suffered was a piece of insubordinate torture devised to remind us that we were pathetic little one-pippers and less than the dust beneath the pipe-band's wheels, but I knew that if we were wise we would just grin and bear it. A newly-joined second-lieutenant is, to some extent, fair game. Properly speaking, he has power and dominion over all warrant officers, N.C.O.s and private men, including pipe- and drum-majors, but he had better go cannily in exercising it. He certainly shouldn't start by locking horns with such a venerable and privileged institution as a Highland regimental pipe band.

"You mean we'll have to put up with that . . . that infernal caterwauling every Friday morning?" he cried, massaging his head. "I can't take it! Heavens, man, I play the piano; I can't afford to be rendered tone-deaf. Look what happened to Beethoven. Anyway, it's . . . it's insubordination, calculated and deliberate. I'm going to complain."

"You're not," I said. "You'll get no sympathy, and it'll only make things worse. Did complaining do Beethoven any good? Just stick your head under the pillow next time, and pretend it's all in the mind."

I soothed him eventually, saw that he got lots of hot, sweet tea (this being the Army's panacea for everything except a stomach wound) and convinced him that we shouldn't say anything about it. This, we discovered, was the attitude of the other subalterns who shared our long bungalow block—which was situated at some distance from the older officers' quarters. Complain, they said, and our superiors would just laugh callously and say it did us good; anyway, for newcomers to a Highland unit to start beefing about the pipe band would probably be some kind of mortal insult. So every Friday morning, with our alarms set at five to six, we just gritted our teeth and waited with towels round our heads, and grimly endured that sudden, appalling blast of sound. Indeed, I developed my own form of retaliation, which was to rise before six, take my ground-sheet and a book out on to the patch of close-cropped weed which passed in North Africa for a lawn, and lie there apparently immersed while the pipe band rendered "Johnnie Cope" with all the stops out a few yards away. When they marched off to wake the rest of the battalion I noticed the pipe-sergeant break ranks, and come over towards me with his pipes under his arm. He was a small, bright-eyed, elfin man whose agility as a Highland dancer was legendary; indeed, my only previous contacts with him had been at twice-weekly morning dancing parades, at which he taught us younger officers the mysteries of the Highland Fling and foursome reel, skipping among us like a new-roused fawn, crying "one-two-three" and comparing our lumbering efforts to the soaring of golden eagles over Grampian peaks. If that was how he saw us, good luck to him.

"Good morning to you, sir," he said, with his head cocked on one side. "Did you enjoy our wee reveille this morning?"

"Fairly well, thanks, pipey," I said, and closed my book. "A bit patchy here and there, I thought. Some hesitation in the warblers—" I didn't know what a warbler was, except that it was some kind of noise you made on the pipes "—and a bum note every now and then. Otherwise, not bad."

"Not—bad?" He went pale, and then pink, and finally said, with Highland archness: "Would you be a piper yoursel', sir, perhaps?"

"Not a note," I said. "But I've heard 'Johnnie Cope' played by Foden's Motor Works Brass Band."

For a moment I thought he was going to burst, and then he began to grin, and then to laugh, shaking his head.

"By George," said he. "A brass band, hey? Stop you, and I'll use that on Pipe-Major Macdonald, the next time he starts bumming his chat. No' bad, no' bad. And does the ither subalterns enjoy oor serenade?"

"I doubt if they've got my ear for music, pipey. Most of them probably think that if you played 'Too Long in this Condition' it would be more appropriate."

He opened his eyes at that. "Too Long in this Condition" is a pibroch, long and weird and full of allusions to the MacCrimmons, and not the kind of thing that ignorant subalterns are expected to know about.

"Aye-aye, weel," he said, smiling. "And you're Mr

MacNeill, aren't you? D Company, if I remember. Ah-
huh. Chust so." He regarded me brightly, nodded, and
turned away. "Look in at the office sometime, Mr Mac-
Neill, if you have the inclination. Chust when you're
passing, you understand."

And that small conversation was a step forward—a
bigger one, really, than playing for the company football team, or getting my second pip as a full lieutenant,
or even crossing the undefined line of acceptance by my
own platoon—which I did quite unintentionally one
night by losing my temper and slinging a mutinous Jock
physically out of the canteen, in defiance of all common
sense, military discipline, and officer-like conduct. For
the pipey and I were friends from that morning on, and
it is no small thing to be friends with a pipe-sergeant
when you are trying to find your nervous feet in a
Highland regiment.

He was in fact subordinate to the pipe-major and the
drum-major, who were the executive heads of the band,
but in his way he carried more weight than either of
them. He was the musician, the authority on air and
march and pibroch, the arbiter when it came to any
question of quality in music or dancing. Years at his
trade had left him with a curious deformity in which
the facial muscles had given way on one side, so that
when he blew, his cheek expanded like a balloon—an
unnerving sight until you got used to it. He had enormous energy, both in movement and conversation, and
was never still, buzzing about like a small tartan wasp,
as when he was instructing young pipers in the finer
points of their art.

"God be kind to me!" he would exclaim, leaping
nervously round some perspiring youth who was going
red in the face over the intricacies of "Wha'll be King
but Cherlie". "You're not plowing up a pluidy palloon,

Wilson! You're summoning the clans for the destruction of the damned Hanovers, aren't you? Your music is charming the claymore out of the thatch and the dirk from the peat, so it is! Now, tuck it into your oxter and wake the hills with your challenge! Away you go!"

And the piper would squint, red-faced, and send his ear-splitting notes echoing off the band-room walls, very creditably, it seemed to me, and the pipey would call on the shades of the great MacCrimmon and Robin Oig to witness the defilement of their heritage.

"It's enuff to make the Celtic aura of my blood turn to effluent!" was one of his more memorable observations. "It's a gathering of fighting men you're meant to be inspiring, boy! The noise you're makin' wouldnae collect a parcel of Caithness tinkers. You'll be swinging it, next! Uplift yourself, Wilson! Mind, it's not bobby-soxers you're tryin' to attract, it's the men of might from the ends of the mountains, with their bonnets down and their shoes kicked off for the charge. And again—give your bags a heeze and imagine you're sclimming up the Heights of Abraham with Young Simon's caterans at your back and the French in front of you, not puffing and wheezing oot some American abomination at half-time at a futball match!"

And eventually, when it had been played to his satisfaction he would beam, and cry:

"There! There's Wilson the Piper, waking the echoes in majesty before the face of kings, and the Chermans aall running away. Now, put up your pipes, and faall oot before you spoil it."

This was his enclosed, jealously-guarded world; he had known nothing else since his boy service—except, as he said himself, "a wee bitty war". Pipers, unlike most military bandsmen, tend to be fighting soldiers; in one Highland unit which I visited in Borneo only a few years ago, the band claimed to have accounted for more Communist terrorists than any of the rifle companies. And in peacetime they were privileged people, with their own little family inside the regiment itself, and the pipey presided over his domain of chanters and reeds and dirks and rehearsals and dancing, and kept a bright eye cocked at the battalion generally, to make sure that tradition was observed and custom honoured, and that there was no falling off in what he would describe vaguely as "Caledonia". If he hadn't been such a decent wee man, he would undoubtedly have been a "professional Highlander" of the most offensive kind.

The only time anyone ever saw the pipe-sergeant anything but thoroughly self-assured and bursting with musical confidence was once every two months or so, when he would produce a new pipe-tune of his own composition, and submit it, in a state bordering on nervous hysteria, to the Colonel, with a request that it might be included in the next beating of Retreat.

"Which one is it this time, pipey?" the Colonel would ask. "'The Mist-Covered Streets of Aberdeen' or 'The 92nd's Farewell to Hogg Market, Calcutta'?"

The pipey would scowl horribly, and then hurriedly arrange his face in what he supposed was a sycophantic grin, and say:

"Ach, you're aye joshing, Colonel, sir. It's jist a wee thing that I thought of entitling 'Captain Lachlan Chisholm's Fancy', in honour of our medical officer. It has a certain . . . och, a captivatin' sense of the bens and the glens and the heroes, sir—a kind of . . . eh . . . miasma, as it were—at least, I think so."

"Does it sound like a pipe-tune?" the Colonel would ask. "If so, by all means play it. I'm sure it will be perfectly splendid."

And at Retreat, with the pipey in a frenzy of excitement, the band would perform, and afterwards the pipey would approach the Colonel and inquire:

"How did you like 'Captain Lachlan Chisholm's Fancy', Colonel, sir?"

And the Colonel, leaning on his cromach, would say:

"Which one was that?"

"The second last, sir—before 'Cock o' the North'."

"Oh, that one. But that was 'Bonnie Dundee', surely? At least, it sounded like 'Bonnie Dundee'. Come to think of it, pipey, your last composition—what was it?—'The Unloading of the 75th at Colaba Causeway', or something—it sounded terribly like 'Highland Laddie'. Of course, I haven't got your musical ear . . ."

"And he can say that again, and a third time in Gaelic," the pipey would rage in the band-room afterwards. "God preserve us from a commanding officer that has no more music than a Border Leicester ewe! 'The Unloading of the 75th', says he—dam' cheek, when fine he knows it was caalled 'The Wild Green Hills of—of—of—ach, where the hell was it, now . . .'"

"Gorbals Cross," the pipe-major would suggest.

"No such thing! And, curse him, he says my composeetions sound like 'Bonnie Dundee' and 'Highland Laddie', as if I wass some penny-whistle street-musician hawkin' my tinny for coppers along Union Street. Stop you, and I'll fix his duff wan o' these days. I'll write a jazz tune, and get it called 'Colonel J. G. F. Gordon's Delight', and have it played in aall the dance-halls! He'll be sorry then!"

And yet, there was no one in the battalion who knew the Colonel better than the pipey did, or was more expert in dealing with that tough, formidable, wise old commanding officer. The truth was that in some things,

especially his love for his regiment, the wily Colonel
could be surprisingly innocent, and the pipey knew just
where and when to touch the hidden nerve.

As in the case of Private Crombie, which would have
sent our modern Race Relations Board into screaming
fits of indignation.

He was in my platoon, one of a draft which joined the
battalion from the Liverpool Scottish. They were
fascinating in their way—men with names like Mac-
Gregor and Cameron and MacPherson, and all with
Scouse accents you could have cut with a knife. Genuine
Liverpool Scots, in fact, sons and grandsons of men who
had settled on Merseyside, totally Lancashire in everything but name and race. But even among them, Private
Crombie stood out as something special. He was what
used to be called a Negro.

Which would not have mattered in the least, but he
also happened to be a piper. And when he marched into
company office about three days after he joined, and
asked if he could apply to join the battalion pipes and
drums, I confess it came as a shock. No doubt it was all
the fault of my bad upbringing, or the dreadful climate
of the 1940s, but my immediate (unspoken) reaction
was: we can't have him marching in the pipe-band, out
in the open with everyone looking. We just can't.

I maintain that this was not what is called race
prejudice, or application of the colour bar. It was, as it
appeared to me, a sense of fitness. If he had been eight
feet tall, or three feet short, I'd have thought the same
thing—simply, that he would have looked out of place
in a Highland regimental pipe-band. But that, obviously,
was something that could not be said. I asked him what
his qualifications were.

He had those, all right. His father had taught him the
pipes—which side of his family was black and which

white, if either was, I never discovered. He had some
sort of proficiency certificate, too, which he laid on my
desk. He was a nice lad, and painfully keen to join the
band, so I did exactly what I would have done in anyone else's case, and said I would forward his application
to the pipe-major; my own approval and the company
commander's went without saying, because it was understood that the band, or any other specialist department,
got first crack at a qualified man. He marched out,
apparently well pleased, Sergeant Telfer and I looked
at each other, said "Aye" simultaneously, and awaited
developments.

What happened was that the pipe-major was on
weekend leave, so Crombie appeared for examination
before the pipe-sergeant, who concealed whatever
emotion he felt, and asked him to play.

"I swear to God, Mr MacNeill," he told me an hour
later, "I hoped he would make a hash of it. Maybe I was
wrong to think that, for the poor lad cannae help bein'
a nigger, but I thought . . . well, if he's a bauchle I'll be
able to turn him doon wi' a clear conscience. Weel, I'm
punished for it, because I cannae. He's a good piper."
He looked me in the eye across the table, and repeated:
"He's a good piper."

"So, what'll you do?"

"I'll have to tell the pipe-major he's fit for admeession.
He's fitter than half the probationers I've got, and that's
the truth. I chust wish to God he was white—or no' so
black, anyway."

Remember that this was almost thirty years ago, and
there have been many changes since then. Also remember that Highland regiments, being strongly national
institutions, are sensitive as to their composition (hence
the old music-hall joke on the lines of: "'Issacstein?'
'Present, sir'. 'O'Flaherty?' 'Present, sir'. Woinarowski?'

'Present, sir'. Right—Cameron Highlanders present and correct, sir.' ")

Carefully, I asked:

"Does his colour matter?"

"You tell me, sir. What'll folk think, if they see our pipe-band some day, on Princes Street, and him as black as the ace o' spades, oot front, in a kilt and bunnet, blawin' away?"

I could pretend that I rejected this indignantly, like a properly enlightened liberal, but I didn't. I saw his point, and I'd have been a hypocrite if I'd tried to dismiss it out of hand. Anyway, there were more practical matters to consider. What would the pipe-major say? What, if it came to that—and it would—would the Colonel say?

The pipe-major, returning on Monday, was in no doubts. He wasn't having a black piper, not if the man was the greatest gift to music that God ever made. The pipey, genuinely distressed, for he was torn between his sense of fitness on the one hand, and an admiration for Crombie's ability on the other, asked the pipe-major to give the lad an audition. The pipe-major, who didn't want to be seen to be operating a colour bar, conceived that here was a way out. He listened to Crombie, told him to fall out—and then made the mistake of telling the pipe-sergeant he didn't think the boy was good enough. That did it.

"No' good enough!" The pipey literally danced in front of my table. "Tellin' *me*, that's been pipin'—aye, and before royalty, too, Balmoral and all—since before Pipe-Major MacDonald had enough wind to belch oot his mither's milk, that my judgement is at fault! By chings, we've lived tae see the day, haven't we chust! No' good enough! I'm tellin' you, Mr MacNeill, that young Crombie iss a piper! And that's that. And fine I know MacDonald iss chust dead set against the poor loon because he's as black as my boot! And from a MacDonald, too," he went on, in a fine indignant irrelevance, "ass if the MacDonalds had anything to hold up their heids aboot—a shower of Argyllshire wogs is what they are! And anither—"

"Hold on, pipey," I said. "Pipe-Major MacDonald is just taking the line you took yourself—what's it going to look like, and what will people think?"

"Beside the point, sir! I'm no' havin' it said that I cannae tell a good piper when I hear one. That boy's good enough for the band, and so I'll tell the Colonel himself!"·

And he did, in the presence of Pipe-Major Mac-Donald, myself (as Crombie's platoon commander), the second-in-command (as chief technical adviser), the Regimental Sergeant-Major (as leading authority on precedent and tradition), and the Adjutant (as one who wasn't going to be left out of such a splendid crisis and scandal). And the pipe-major, who had the courage of his convictions, repeated flatly that he didn't think Crombie was good enough, and also that he didn't want a black man in his band, "for the look of the thing". But, being a MacDonald, which is something a shade craftier than a Borgia, he added: "But I'm perfectly happy to abide by your decision, sir."

The Colonel, who had seen through the whole question and back again in the first two minutes, looked from the pipe-major to the pipey, twisted his greying moustache, and remarked that he took the pipe-major's point. He (the Colonel) had never seen a white man included in a troop of Zulu dancers, and he'd have thought it looked damned odd if he had.

The Adjutant, who had a happy knack of being contentious, observed that, on the other hand, he'd never

heard of a white chap who *wanted* to join a troop of
Zulu dancers, and would they necessarily turn him
down if one (a white chap, that was) applied for
membership?

The Colonel observed that he, the Colonel, wasn't a
bloody Zulu, so he wasn't in a position to say.

The second-in-command remarked that the Gurkhas
had pipe bands; damned good they were, too.

The Colonel looked at the R.S.M. "Mr Mackintosh?"

This, I thought, would be interesting. In those days
few R.S.M.s had university degrees, or much education
beyond elementary school, but long experience, and
what you can only call depth of character, had given
them considerable judicial wisdom; if I were on trial for
murder, I'd as soon have R.S.M. Mackintosh on the
bench as any judge in the land. He stood thoughtful for
a moment, six and a quarter feet of kilted, polished
splendour, and then inclined his head with massive
dignity towards the Colonel.

"It seems to me, sir," he said carefully, "that we have
a difference of expert opeenion. The pipe-sergeant holds
that this soldier is a competent piper; the pipe-major
considers he is nott. But, not bein' an expert mysel', I
don't know what standard is required of a probationary
piper?" And he looked straight at the pipe-major, who
frowned.

"The boy's no' that bad," he conceded. "But . . . but
he'll look gey queer on parade, sir."

The second-in-command said that you couldn't put a
square peg in a round hole. Not unless you forced it,
anyway, in his experience.

The Adjutant said someone would be sure to make a
joke about the Black Watch. Which, since we weren't
the Black Watch, would be rather pointless, of course,
but still . . .

The Colonel said the Adjutant could stop talking rot, and get back to the point, which was whether Crombie was or was not a fit and proper person to be admitted to the pipe band. It seemed to the Colonel that, in spite of the pipe-major's reservations about his proficiency, there was no reason why Crombie couldn't achieve a satisfactory standard ...

The second-in-command said that many black chaps were, in point of fact, extremely musical. Chap Armstrong, for example. Not that the second-in-command was particularly partial to that kind of music.

The Adjutant opened his mouth, thought better of it, and the Colonel went on to say that it wasn't a man's fault what colour his skin was; on the other hand, it wasn't anyone's fault that a pipe band was expected to present a certain appearance. There he paused, and then the pipe-sergeant, who had held his peace until the time was ripe, said:

"Aye, right enough. Folk would laugh at us."

The Colonel, without thinking, said stiffly: "Oh? Who?"

"Oh . . . folk, sir," said the pipey. "People . . . and ither regiments . . . might . . ."

The Colonel looked at him, carefully, and you could see that the die was cast. It wasn't that the Colonel could be kidded by the pipey; he wasn't the kind of simpleton who would say "Damn what other people and other regiments think, Crombie is going to play in the pipe band, and that's that." But if he now made the *opposite* decision, he might be thought to be admitting that perhaps he *did* care what other people thought. It was a very nice point, in a delicately balanced question, the pipey had just made it a little more tricky for him, and both the Colonel and the pipey knew it.

"Mr Mackintosh?" said the Colonel at length, and

everyone knew he was looking for confirmation. He got it.

"The pipe-major, sir, describes Crombie as nott bad," said the R.S.M. slowly. "The pipe-sergeant says he is good. So I take it he can qualify as a probationary piper. That bein' so—we've taken him as a soldier. Whatever work he's suited for, he should be given. If he's fit to march in a rifle company, I'm poseetive he's fit to march in the pipes and drums." And again he looked at the pipe-major.

"Good," said the Colonel, and because he was an honest man he added: "I'm relieved. I'd not have cared to be the man who told Crombie the band couldn't take him. I've no doubt he knows exactly how good a piper he is."

And Crombie played in the pipe-band—having been admitted for all the wrong reasons, no doubt. I'm perfectly certain that the Colonel, the pipe-major, and the pipe-sergeant (in his own perverse way) wished that he just wasn't there, because he *did* look odd, in that day and age, and there's no use pretending he didn't. Although, as the second-in-command remarked, some people probably thought that a pipe-band looked a pretty odd thing in the first place; some people thought it *sounded* odd, too—not as odd as those bands one saw at the cinema, though, with the chap Armstrong and fellows called Duke and Earl something-or-other. Probably not titled men at all, he suspected.

Personally, I was glad about Crombie. It wasn't just that I felt the same way as the R.S.M. (that deep and mysterious man), but that I could see that Crombie loved what he was doing, and was good at it. And when I review my memories of that pipe-band now, thirty years on, I don't think of Crombie at all, which probably proves something. Mention "pipers" to me, and my

immediate recollection is of "Johnnie Cope", and the
way they used to batter our ear-drums on a Friday at
dawn.

Incidentally, that peculiar little bit of subaltern-
baiting came to an abrupt end, thanks to the cunning of
Lieutenant Mackenzie, in a week when I was out on
detachment. It seems that the Colonel stayed late in the
mess one Thursday night, his wife being away in Cairo,
and yarned on with the subalterns in the ante-room until
after two in the morning. And being too tired to make
the two-mile drive home to the married quarters, he
accepted the suggestion of Mackenzie that he stay over
for the night—in a vacant room in the subalterns'
quarters. So the Colonel borrowed a pair of pyjamas
and burrowed in for the night, remarking cheerfully
that he hoped he'd sleep as soundly as he used to do
when he, too, was a one-pipper with not a care in the
world.

"And he did, too—until precisely 6 a.m.," Mackenzie
informed me later. "And then the pipey and his gang
sneaked up, as usual, and took deep breaths, and started
blowing the bloody roof off, right outside the old boy's
kip. I've never," Mackenzie went on contentedly,
"actually seen a hungry vulture with a fire-cracker tied
to its leg. And, brother, I don't need to. He came out of
that room like Krakatoa erupting, fangs bared and
blood in his eye. I'd no idea the old man could shift like
that. And I'll bet you've never seen an entire pipe band
in full flight, either—not just retreating, but running
like hell, and somebody with his foot through the big
drum. If the Colonel hadn't been in bare feet, he'd have
caught someone, and there'd have been murder done.
Anyway, when the smoke had cleared, he was understood to say that the pipe-band could henceforth sound
'Johnnie Cope' on the other side of the barracks, round

Support Company, and if they ever set foot within two hundred yards of any officers' quarters again, he, personally, would reorganise them in several unusual ways. This is an edited version, of course. And that," concluded Mackenzie smugly, "is the pipey's eye on a plate. Thank your clever old Kenny. We'll sleep in peace on Fridays after this."

Strangely enough, we didn't. Probably we were suffering from withdrawal symptoms, but Friday reveille, with only the distant drift of the band, found us fractious and peevish. Even my room-mate said he missed it, rather; he liked the bit where the drummers crashed out their tattoo at the beginning, it made him feel all martial, he said. We didn't actually go the length of asking the band to come back, but there was no doubt of it, Friday wasn't the same any more.

The only time I heard them beat reveille outside the subalterns' quarters again was a long time after, when we had moved back to Edinburgh, and the old Colonel had gone. It was on my last Friday in the Army, just before I was demobilised, and I like to think it was the pipey's farewell gift. It had all the old effect—I finished up against the far wall, thrashing feebly in a state of shock, while "Johnnie Cope" came thundering in like a broadside. I had a new room-mate by this time, a stranger to the battalion, and when he could make himself heard he announced his intention—he was a large, aggressive young man—of going out and putting an immediate stop to it.

"Don't you dare," I shouted above the din. "Let them alone. And think yourself privileged."

Nowadays, in middle age, I'm accustomed to waking up in the ordinary way, with a slightly fuzzy feeling, and a vague discontent, and my old broken shoulder aching, and twinges in my calves and ankles. And sometimes, if my thoughts turn that way, I can think smugly that one of the compensations nowadays is that there are no tables to scrub, or men of ill-will hitting the coal-bucket with the poker, or hounding me out into the ablutions through the snow—and then I feel sad, because never again will I hear "Johnnie Cope" in the morning.

General knowledge, private information

All my life I have been plagued by a marvellous memory for totally useless information. Probably no other human being now alive could tell you (or would want to, for that matter), all in one breath, that the woman in whose coal cellar Guy Fawkes hid his explosives was called Mrs Bright, that Casanova, Charlemagne, and Hans Andersen were all born on 2 April, and that Schopenhauer couldn't abide carters cracking whips beneath his bedroom window. And add, for good measure, the names of the Oxford batsmen who succumbed to Cobden's devastating hat-trick in the University match of 1870.

You get no marks for knowing these things, as people were always telling me at school. Other children knew the subjunctive of *moneo,* and exactly where to drop the perpendicular in Pythagoras, how to dissect an adverbial clause (I didn't even know what an adverb was, and don't push me even now), and how to do volumetric analysis. They absorbed these matters without difficulty, and poured them out on to paper at examinations, while I sat pathetically, having scrawled my name, and the number "1" in the margin, wondering if the examiners would allow me anything for knowing that the ice-cream Chico Marx sold in *A Day at the Races* was "tutsi-fruitsi", and that there was an eighteenth-century buccaneer who became Archbishop of York, that the names of the *Bounty*'s quartermasters were Norton and Lenkletter, or that Martin Luther suffered from piles.

It wasn't even respectable general knowledge, and heaven knows I tried to forget it, along with the identities of the playing cards in Wild Bill Hickok's hand when he was shot, the colours of all the football teams in the old Third Division (Northern Section), and the phrase for "Do you surrender?" in the language which Tarzan spoke to the apes. But it still won't go away. And an exhaustive knowledge of utter rubbish is not a social asset (ask anyone who has been trapped next to me at a party) or of more than limited use in keeping up with a television quiz show. Mr Gascoigne's alert, glittering-eyed young men, bristling with education, jab at their buzzers and rattle out streams of information on Sumerian architecture and Gregorian music and the love poetry of John Donne while I am heaving about in my armchair with my mouth full, knocking over tea-cups and babbling frantically: "Wait, wait!—King's Evil! No, no, dammit—the other thing that Shelley's nurse died of—didn't she?—No, wait—Dr Johnson—or Lazarus—or, or what's his name?—in that play—not bloody Molière!—hang on, it's coming! The . . . the other one—with the drunk grandee who thinks he's somebody's father . . ."

And by then they are on to Hindemith or equestrian statues at Sinigaglia. It is no consolation to be able to sit growling jealously that there isn't one of them who could say who it was that Captain Kidd hit over the head with a bucket, or what it was that Claude Rains dropped into a wastepaper basket in the film *Casablanca*

—and then memory of a different kind takes hold, and I am back in the tense and smoky atmosphere of the Uaddan Canteen, sweating heavily on the platform with the other contestants, and not a murmur from the Jocks and Fusiliers packed breathlessly waiting in the body of the hall, with a two-pound box of Turkish Delight and the credit of the regiment to play for, as the question-master adjusts his spectacles, fixes me with a malevolent smile, and asks:

"What were the names of the five seventeenth-century statesmen whose initials made up the word 'Cabal'?"

There are no such general knowledge quizzes nowadays—and no such sublimely-inspired authorities as Private McAuslan, savant, sage, universal man, and philosopher extraordinary. For reviewing his long, un-soldierly, and generally insanitary career, I'd say that that was McAuslan's big moment, when he rose above his unseemly self and stood forth whole, a bag of chips in his hand and the divine fire of revelation in his mind.

If you doubt this, I can only tell you that I was there and saw it happen. But to explain it properly, and obtain a true perspective, I have to go back a few days earlier to the battalion concert which, along with the Colonel's liver, was the origin of the whole thing.

If you have attended a battalion concert in an overseas garrison you will know that they are, theatrically speaking, unique—and not merely because nothing works, including the curtain. The whole production is ill-conceived and badly under-rehearsed to begin with, half the cast have to be press-ganged into appearance, the standard of performance would shame a kindergarten pantomime, the piano is untuned, the lighting intermittent, C Company's tenor (who thinks he is Scotland's answer to Gigli) butchers his way through "Ave Maria" and "Because God made thee mine" to demented applause from the sentimental soldiery, one of the storemen does conjuring tricks with a pullthrough and pieces of four-by-two cleaning cloth, the idiot Lieutenant MacNeill, shuffling and crimson with embarrassment, does his supposedly comic monologue and dies standing up, the Adjutant, who is prompting in the wings, loses his script and puts the entire stage-crew under close arrest in a voice shrill with hysteria while the audience roars "Encore", and everybody on the safe side of the footlights loves it. Except the Colonel.

This is because he is stuck in the middle of the front row, surrounded by all the visiting brass and their wives, and knowing that the climax to the whole terrible show, which his soldiery are waiting for like knitting-women impatient for the tumbril, will be the moment when the battalion funny-man comes on and does the court-jester bit. Our own local comedian was an evil and disreputable Glasgow keelie called McCann, the scruff of A Company, and generally regarded as that unit's answer to Private McAuslan. He came bauchling confidently on, his wits honed by years of abusing referees, policemen and tram conductors, convulsed the hoi-polloi with his grating catch-phrase ("Hullaw rerr, fellas, see's a knife, Ah wantae cut up a side street"), and set the tone by winking at the Colonel and addressing him affably as "china".

Thereafter, with delicately edged allusion and innuendo, he took the mickey out of his commanding officer in a performance judged with such a niceness that it stopped just a shaved inch short of outright insubordination. It really was masterly, in its way, and would have won plaudits from Will Kemp and Archie Armstrong, who would have expected to go to the Tower, if not the block, for it. And the Colonel, pipe clenched in his teeth, took it with an eager, attentive smile that promised penalties unmentionable for Private McCann if ever he was damnfool enough to get himself wheeled into the orderly room on a charge.

The last act of the evening, after McCann had bounced off to tumultuous applause (with the Colonel clapping grimly and regularly) was a complete anti-climax. It was a general knowledge test among teams from the six companies, devised by the Padre, and it laid the expected theatrical egg, with the mob streaming away to the canteen before it was finished. But the Colonel sat it out, and was heard to say in the mess afterwards that it had been the only decent event on the programme. Presumably anything looked good to him after McCann.

"The rest of it," he observed to the Fusilier Colonel, who had been an interested (and, during McCann's turn, an inwardly delighted) guest, "was just bloody awful. Of a piece with all modern entertainment, of course. Haven't had a decent film, even, since *Snow White*. At least these general knowledge quizzes serve some useful purpose—anything does that imparts information to the men. God knows most of 'em could do with some educa-tion, considering the drivel that's served up to them as ntertainment." And he had the crust to scowl at me— which, considering he had dragooned me into the show in the first place ("A good officer ought to take part in all his men's activities; give 'em your monologue"), was pretty cool, I thought.

The Fusilier Colonel said he doubted if the general knowledge competition we had heard that night was very educational; it had consisted, he pointed out, of questions mostly about sport.

"Nothing wrong with that," said our Colonel. "Shows a healthy outlook. Have another gin."

"Thanks," said the Fusilier Colonel. "What I meant

was, to be really useful a general knowledge quiz ought to be more broadly based, don't you think? I mean—football and racing are all very well, but general knowledge should take in, well, art, politics, literature, that sort of thing." He took a sip of his gin and added: "Perhaps your Jocks aren't interested, though."

That, as they say, did it. But for McCann, and the fact that our Colonel's liver must have been undergoing one of its periodic spells of mutinous behaviour, he'd probably just have grunted agreement. As it was, he stopped short in the act of refuelling his pipe and asked the Fusilier Colonel what the devil he meant. The Fusilier Colonel said, nothing, really, but general knowledge quizzes ought to be about general knowledge. They'd had one in his battalion, and he'd been astonished at how much his chaps—quite ordinary chaps, he'd always thought—knew about all sorts of things.

Our Colonel did a brief, thoughtful quiver, looked across the mess with that chin-up, faraway stare that his older comrades associated with the Singapore siege, and said, was that so, indeed. He finished filling his pipe, and you could see him wondering whether the Fusilier Colonel had somehow managed to enlist the entire Fellowship of All Souls in his battalion. Then he looked round, and if ever a man was taking inventory of his own unit's intellectual powers, he was doing it then. There was the Padre, with an M.A. (Aberdeen), and the M.O. with presumably some scientific knowledge—pretty well versed in fishing, anyway—and then his eye fell on me, and I knew what he was thinking. A few days before he'd heard me—out of that fund of my trivia—explaining to the Adjutant, who was wrestling futilely with a crossword, that the term "derrick" derived from the name of an Elizabethan hangman. Eureka, he was thinking.

"Tell you what," he said to the Fusilier Colonel. "How'd you like to have one of these quiz competitions —between our battalions? Just for interest, eh?"

"All right," said the Fusilier Colonel. "A level fiver?"

"Done," said our Colonel, promptly, and in that fine spirit of philosophic inquirers bent on the propagation of knowledge for its own sake they proceeded to hammer out the rules, conditions and penalties under which the contest would be conducted. It took them three double whiskies and about half a pint of gin, and the wheeling and dealing would have terrified Tammany Hall. But finally they agreed that the two teams, four men strong, should be drawn from all ranks of the respective battalions, that the questions should be devised independently by the area education officer, that the local Roman Catholic padre should act as umpire (our Colonel teetered apprehensively over that, and presumably concluded that the Old Religion was marginally closer to our cause—Jacobites, Glasgow Irish, and all that—than to the Fusiliers'), and that the contest should be held in a week's time on neutral ground, namely the Uaddan Canteen. And when, with expressions of mutual good will, the Fusilier Colonel and his party had left, our Colonel called for another stiff one, mopped his balding brow, refilled his pipe, and took the operation in hand. He formed the Padre and myself into an O-Group, with the Adjutant co-opted as an adviser, told the rest of the mess to shut up or go to bed, announced: "Now, this is the form," and paced to and fro like Napoleon before Wagram, plotting his strategy. Dividing his discourse under the usual subheadings—object, information, personnel, communications, supply, and transport—he laid it all on the line.

"These Fusiliers," he said, smoking thoughtfully. "Probably quite brainy. Never can tell, of course, but

they put up a dam' fine show at Anzio, and Colonel
Fenwick is nobody's fool. Don't be discouraged by the
fact that they've had one or two of their chaps through
Staff College—the kind of idiot who can write p.s.c.
after his name these days is, to my mind, quite unfit for
brain-work of any kind and usually has to be excused
boots." The Colonel had not been to Staff College.
"However, we can't afford to take 'em lightly. Their
recruiting area is the north-east of England, which I
grant you is much like the Australian outback with coal-
mines added, but we can't count too much on that.
There's a university thereabouts—which reminds me,
Michael, we'll have to check on where this area education officer hails from. The chap who's setting the
questions. Fenwick proposed him—bigod, I'll bet he's a
Geordie—"

"He's a Cornishman," said the Adjutant. "Pen-pal, or
some such name."

"Thank God for that," said the Colonel. "You're sure?
Right, then, we come to our own team. You, Padre, and
you, young Dand, will select as your team-mates the
two most informed, alert and intelligent men in the
battalion. Officers or other ranks, I don't care which—
but understand, I want a team who can answer the
questions put to them clearly, fully, and accurately, and
in a soldier-like manner. No dam' shuffling and scratching heads. When a question's asked—crack! straight in
with the answer, like that."

"Provided we know the answer," said the Padre, and
the Colonel looked at him like a dyspeptic vulture.

"This battalion," he said flatly, "knows all the answers.
Understand? What's the shortest book in the Bible?"

"Third John," said the Padre automatically.

"There you are, you see," said the Colonel, shrugging
in the grand manner. "It's just a matter of alertness and

concentration. And—training." He wagged his pipe impressively. "Some form of training is absolutely essential, to ensure that you and the rest of the team are at a highly-tuned pitch on the night of the contest. The questions are to fall under the headings of general knowledge; art and literature and music and what-not; politics; and sport. I suppose," he went on reflectively, "that you could read a bit . . . but don't for God's sake go swotting feverishly and upsetting yourselves. Some chaps at Wellington used to, I remember—absolutely hopeless on the day. I," he added firmly, "never swotted. Just stayed off alcohol for twenty-four hours in advance, went for a walk, had a bath and a good sleep, a light breakfast . . . well, here I am. So just keep your digestions regular, no late hours, and perhaps brush up a bit with . . . well, with some of those general knowledge questions in the *Sunday Post*. I don't doubt the education officer will draw heavily on those. Anyway, they'll get you into the feel of the thing. Apart from that—any suggestions?"

The Adjutant said he had a copy of *Whitaker's Almanack* in the office, if that was any use.

"Excellent," said the Colonel. "That's the sort of practical approach we need. Very good, Michael. No doubt there's some valuable stuff in the battalion library, too." (I knew of nothing, personally, unless one hoped to study social criminology through the medium of *No Orchids for Miss Blandish* or *Slay-ride for Cutie*.)

"And that," said the Colonel, ordering up four more big ones, "is that. It's just a question of preparation, and we'll have this thing nicely wrapped up. I've every confidence, as usual—" he gave us his aquiline beam "—and I feel sure that you have, too. We'll show the Fusiliers where the brain-power lies."

The trouble with the Colonel, you see. was that he'd

been spoiled by success. Whether it was taking and
holding a position in war, or thrashing all opposition at
football, or looking better than anyone else on ceremonial parades, or even a question of the battalion's
children topping the prize-list at the garrison school, he
expected no less than total triumph. And perhaps because he so trustingly expected it, he usually got it—
and a trifle over. It was a subtle kind of blackmail, in a
way, and that crafty old soldier knew just how to
operate it. Leadership they call it.

I've seen it manifest itself in most curious ways, as
when the seven-year-old daughter of Sergeant Allison
was taking a ballet examination in Edinburgh—and
there, just before it began, was the Colonel, in tweeds
and walking-stick, just looking in, you understand, to
see that all was in order, gallantly chatting up the
young instructresses in their leotards, playing the genial
old buffer and missing nothing, and then giving the
small and tremulous Miss Allison a wink and a growling
whisper before stalking off to his car. The fact was, the
man was as nervous as her parents, because she was part
of his regimental family. "He'll be there at the Last
Judgement," the M.O. once said, "cadging a light off
St Peter so that he can whisper 'This is one of my Jocks
coming in, by the way . . .'"

It followed that the quiz against the Fusiliers assumed
an importance that it certainly didn't deserve, and I
actually found myself wondering if I ought to try to
read right through the *Britannica* beforehand. Fortunately common sense reasserted itself, and I concen-
trated instead on selecting the remaining two members
of the team—the Padre insisted that was my affair; he
was going to be too busy praying.

Actually, it wasn't difficult. The Padre and I had
agreed that in the quiz he would deal with questions

on what, in a moment of pure Celtic pessimism, he irritably described as "the infernal culture"—that is, literature, music and the arts—while I would look after the general knowledge. So we needed a political expert and a sporting one. The political expert was easy, I said: it could only be Sergeant McCaw, Clydeside Communist and walking encyclopedia on the history of capitalist oppression and the emergence of the Working Man.

The Padre was horrified. "Ye daren't risk it! The man's a Bolshevik, and he's cost me more members than Sunday opening. He'll use the occasion for spouting red propaganda—man, Dandy, the Colonel'll go berserk!"

"He's about the only man in this battalion whose knowledge of Parliament goes beyond the label of an H.P. sauce bottle," I said. "It would be criminal not to pick him—he can even tell you what the Corn Laws were."

"Is that right?" said the Padre, metaphorically pulling his shawl round his shoulders. "I fear the worst. Stop you till he starts calling Churchill a fascist bully gorged on the blood of the masses. What about sport?"

"Forbes," I said. "From my platoon. He's the man."

"Yon? He's chust a troglodyte."

"Granted," I said, "but if you knew your Reasons Annexed as well as he knows his league tables, you'd be Moderator by now." And in the face of his doubts I summoned Private Forbes—small, dark, and sinful, and the neatest inside forward you ever saw.

"Forbes," I said. "Who holds the record for goals scored in a first-class match?"

He didn't even blink. "Petrie, Arbroath, got thirteen against Aberdeen Bon-Accord in 1889. He wis playin' ootside right, an'—"

"Right," I said. "Who got most in a league game?"

"Joe Payne, o' Chelsea, got ten when he was playin' fur—"

"What's the highest individual score in first-class cricket?"

"Bradman, the Australian, he got 452 in a State game—"

"How many Britons have held the world heavyweight title?"

"None." He took a breath. "Bob - Fitzsimmons - wis - English - but - he - was - namerrican - citizen - when - he - beat - Corbett - an' - Toamy - Burns - wis - a - Canadian - but - that - disnae - count - an'—"

"Fall out, Forbes, and thank you," I said, and looked at the Padre, who was sitting slightly stunned. "Well?"

He sighed. "When you consider the power of the human brain, ye feel small," he began, and I could see that we were going to be off shortly on another fine philosophic Hebridean flight. So I left him, and went to find Sergeant McCaw and confirm his selection.

The next week was just ridiculous. You'd have thought the Jocks wouldn't even be interested in such an arcane and contemptible business as an inter-regimental general knowledge competition, but they treated it like the World Cup. Scotsmen, of course, if they feel that national prestige is in any way at stake, tend to go out of their minds; tell them there was to be a knitting bee against England and they would be on the touchline shouting "Purl, Wullie! See's the chain-stitch, but!" And as is the case with British regiments anywhere, they and the Fusiliers detested each other heartily. That, and the subtle influence which I'm sure the Colonel percolated through the unit by some magic of his own, was enough to make the quiz the burning topic of the hour.

I first realised this when, during a ten-minute halt on

a short route march, Private Fletcher of the lantern visage and inventive mind mentioned the quiz to me, and observed artlessly, as he borrowed a light: "Would be a' right if ye knew what the questions wis goin' tae be, wouldnit?" Once upon a time I'd have thought this just a silly remark, but I knew my Fletcher by now.

"It would," I said. "But if somebody was to bust into the education officer's premises at night, and start rifling his papers, that wouldn't be all right. Know what I mean?"

"Whit ye take me fur?" He was all hurt surprise. "Ah wis just mentionin'. Passin' the time." He paused. "They say the odds is five tae two against us."

"You mean there's a book being made? And we're not favourites?"

"No kiddin', sur. The word's got roond. See the Padre? He's a wandered man, that; he disnae know what time it is. Ye cannae depend on him."

"He's an intelleck-shul, but," observed Daft Bob Brown.

"Intellectual yer granny. Hear him the ither Sunday? On aboot the Guid Samaritan, an' the Levite passin' by on the ither side, an' whit a helluva shame it wis, tae leave some poor sowel lyin' in the road? Well seen the Padre hasnae been doon Cumberland Street lately. Ah'd dam soon pass by on the ither side. Becos if Ah didnae, Ah ken fine whit I'd get—half a dozen Billy Boys fleein' oot a close tae banjo me."

This naturally led to a theological discussion in which I bore no part; I'd been lured into debate on the fundamentals with my platoon before. Nor was I surprised that they held a poor opinion of the Padre's intellect— he did have a tendency to wander off into a kind of metaphysical trance in the pulpit. Skye man, of course.

But I was intrigued to find that they were interesting themselves in the quiz; even Private McAuslan.

"Whit's an intelleck-shul?" he inquired.

"A clever b——", explained Fletcher, which is not such a bad definition, when you come to think of it. "Don't you worry, dozey," he went on. "It disnae affect you. An intellectual's a fella that can think."

"Ah can think," said McAuslan, aggrieved, and the platoon took him up on it, naturally.

"What wi'?"

"Your brains are in your bum, kid."

"Hey, sir, why don't ye hiv McAuslan in yer quiz team?"

"Aye, he's the wee boy wi' the brains."

"Professor McAuslan, N.B.G., Y.M.C.A. and bar."

"Right—fall in!" I said, for McAuslan's expression had turned from persecuted to murderous. He shuffled into the ranks, informing Fletcher raucously that he could think, him, he wisnae so bluidy dumb, and Fletcher wis awfy clever, wasn't he, etc., etc.

But I hadn't realised quite how gripped they were by quiz fever until I became aware, midway through the week, that I was being taken care of, solicitously, like a heavy-weight in training. I was conscious, in my leisure moments, of being watched; outside my window I heard my orderly say: "It's a' right; he's readin' a book," and on two other occasions he asked pointedly if he could get me anything from the library—a thing he'd never done before. My platoon behaved like Little Lord Fauntleroys, obviously determined to do nothing to disturb the equilibrium of the Great Brain; the Padre complained that he could get no work done for Jocks coming into his office to ask if he was all right, and could they get him anything. Sergeant McCaw, whose feeling for the proletariat did not prevent his being an oppressively efficient martinet with his own platoon, and consequently unpopular, reported that he had actually been brought tea in the morning; he was suspicious, and plainly apprehensive that the jacquerie were about to rise.

It reached a peak on the Thursday, when I was playing in a company football match, and was brought down by one of the opposition. Before I could move he was helping me up—"awfy sorry, sir, ye a'right? It was an accident, honest." And this from a half-back whose normal conduct on the field was that of a maddened clog-dancer.

By the Saturday afternoon I was convinced that if this kind of consideration didn't stop soon, I would go out of my mind. The Padre was feeling it, too—I found him in the mess, muttering nervously, dunking egg-sandwiches in his tea and trying to eat them with a cigarette in his mouth. I believe if I had said anything nice to him or asked him who wrote *The Tenant of Wildfell Hall* he would have burst into tears. The Colonel stalked in, full of fight, shot anxious glances at us, and decided that for once breezy encouragement would be out of place. The Adjutant said hopefully that he'd heard there was a touch of dysentery going round the Fusilier barracks, but on the other hand, he'd also heard that they had a full set of *The Children's Encyclopedia*, so there wasn't much in it, either way, really. You could feel the tension building up as we sat, munching scones; I was getting into a nervous state, and showed it by quoting to the Padre, "I would it were bedtime, Hal, and all well", and he started like a convulsed impala and cried: "Henry the Fourth, Part One! Or is it Part Two? No—Part One!—I think. . . . Oh, dear, dear!" and sank back, rubbing his brow.

It was a relief finally to get to the Uaddan Canteen,

already filled with a light fog of smoke from the troops who packed the big concert hall. The rival factions of supporters had arranged themselves on either side of the centre aisle, so that on one hand the sea of khaki was dotted with the cockades on the caps which the Fusiliers had folded and thrust through their epaulettes, and on the other by dark green tartan shoulder flashes. There were even redcaps at the back of the hall; I found myself wondering whether there had ever been a general knowledge contest in history where they had called in the police even before the start.

In the centre of the front row sat the area commander, a portly, jovial brigadier with his complexion well seasoned by sun and booze, and on either side of him the Colonels, talking across him with a smiling jocularity you could have sliced bread on. Officers of both regiments, plus a few of the usual commissioned strays, made up the first two rows, and immediately behind them on the Highland side I saw the serried ranks of Twelve Platoon, with Private McAuslan to the fore eating chips from a huge, steaming bag with cannibal-like gusto. You could almost smell them on the platform.

All this I observed through a crack in the curtains at the back of the stage, where we and our opponents were briefly assembled, smiling uneasily at each other until we were given the word to file out on to the platform. We came out to a reception reminiscent of a Nuremberg rally which has got out of hand; the Fusiliers thundered their boots on the floor, while stern Caledonia on the other side got up and roared abuse across the aisle, sparing a decibel or two for the encouragement of their team. "There's the wee boys!" I recognised the cry of Private Fletcher, while McAuslan signified his support by standing on his chair and clapping his hands rhythmically above his head—unfortunately he was still holding his supper in one hand, not that he minded; if you're McAuslan, a few chips in your hair is nothing.

We took our places, each side ranged on hard chairs behind two long Naafi tables on either side of the stage, and the question-master, a horn-rimmed young man with a long neck and the blue Education Corps flash on his shoulder, assembled his papers importantly at a little table in between. He was joined by Father Tuohy, the Roman Catholic chaplain, known locally as the Jovial Monk, who mitted the crowd to sustained applause, told a couple of quick stories, exchanged gags with the groundlings, and generally set the scene. (If ever the Palladium needs a compère at the last minute, they can simply engage the nearest military priest; I don't know why, but there never was an R.C. padre yet who couldn't charm the toughest audience into submission.)

Tuohy then explained the rules. There would be individual questions to each man in turn, on his particular subject. If he answered correctly, he got one point and could opt for a second slightly harder question, worth two points, and if again successful, attempt a third still harder question, worth three. If he failed at any stage he kept the points he had, but the question which had stumped him went to the opposition, who scored double if they got it right. At any turn, a contestant could ask for a ten-point question, which would be a real stinker, split into five parts, with two points for each, but unless he got at least four of the parts right, he scored nothing at all. It sounded fairly tricky, with pitfalls waiting for the ambitious.

While he talked, I glanced at our opponents—three officers, one of them a stout, shrewd-looking major, and a bespectacled warrant officer who looked like a Ph.D. and probably was. I glanced along at my companions: Forbes, looking villainous and confident, was sitting up straight with his elbows squared on the board; McCaw, beside him, showed signs of strain on his sallow, tight-skinned face; next to me the Padre was humming the Mingulay boat song between his teeth, his Adam's apple giving periodic leaps, while he gazed up at the big moths fluttering round the lights. It was sweating hot.

"Right," said Father Tuohy, smiling round genially. "All set?" I could glimpse the sea of faces in the hall out of the corner of my eye; I wished I hadn't eaten so many scones, for I was feeling decidedly ill—why? For a mere quiz? Yes, for a mere quiz. There was a muscle fluttering in my knee, and I wanted a drink, but I knew if I picked up the tumbler in front of me I'd drop it in sheer nervousness. Right—I'd play it safe, dead safe; no rash scrambling after points; nice and easy, by ear.

"First general knowledge question to the Fusiliers," said the question-master; he had a rather shrill Home Counties voice. "What is a triptych?"

Well, thank God he hadn't asked me. "Screens" flashed across my mind, but I didn't know, really. Private Fletcher evidently did, though, for in the pause following the question a grating Scottish voice from the body of the hall observed audibly:

"That's a right Catholic question, yon!"

Father Tuohy snorted with amusement, and composed himself while the Fusilier major answered—I don't know what he said, but it earned him a point, and he asked for a second question.

"With whom or what," said the question-master, "was Europa indiscreet—not necessarily on the firing-range?" He smirked, lop-sidedly; ah-ha, I thought, we've got an intellectual joker here.

"A bull," said the major, and looked across at me. I knew what he was thinking; the questions, for an army quiz, were middling tough; if he flunked on the third, would I be able to answer it and net six points? Wisely, at that stage of the game, he passed, and the question-master turned to me, his glasses a-gleam. Easy, easy, I thought, just sit and listen—and then some dreadful automatic devil inside me seized on my tongue and made me say, in a nonchalant croak:

"I'd like a ten-pointer, please."

The Padre actually gave a muted scream and shuddered away from me, the question-master sat up straight, there was a stir on the platform, a gasp from the hall, and then a bay of triumph from Twelve Platoon: "Darkie's the wee boy! Get tore in!" Just for a moment, amidst the horrifying realisation of what I'd done, I felt proud—and then I wanted to be sick. My fiend had prompted me to put on a show, for reasons of pure bravado; if I managed to lift ten points it would be a tremendous psychological start. And if I failed? From the tail of my eye I could see the Colonel; he was clicking his lighter nervously.

"For ten points then," said the question-master, rummaging out another sheaf of papers. "I'm going to give you the names of five famous horses, both real and legendary. For two points each, tell me the names of their owners." He paused impressively, and apart from the subterranean squelching in my throat, there wasn't a sound. "Ronald. Pegasus. Bucephalus. Black Auster. And—" he gave me what looked like a gloating grin "—Incitatus."

Silence in the hall, and then from somewhere in Twelve Platoon a voice said in horrified awe: "Bluidy hell!" The Colonel's lighter clattered on the floor, I felt about two thousand eyes riveted on my sweating face—and relief was flooding over me like a huge wave. Take it easy, I was saying to myself; don't let your tongue betray you. By a most gorgeous fluke, you're in business.

I took a deep breath, tried to keep my voice from shaking, and said:

"In the same order . . . ahm . . . yes . . . the owners . . . er, would be." I paused, determined to get it right. "The Seventh Earl of Cardigan, Bellerophon, Alexander the Great, Titus Herminius—in Macaulay's 'Lays'—and the Roman Emperor Caligula."

Forgive me for describing it, but in a life that has had its share of pursed lips, censorious glares, and downright abuse and condemnation, there haven't been many moments like that one. It rocked the hall, although I say it myself. The question-master, torn between admiration and resentment at seeing one of his prize questions hammered into the long grass, stuttered, and said: "Right! Ten points—yes, ten points!", the front two rows applauded briskly, the Fusilier major shaded his face with his hand and said something to the man next him, and Twelve Platoon threw up their sweaty nightcaps with abandon. ("Gi' the ba' tae Darkie! Aw-haw-hey! Whaur's yer triptyches noo?" etc.) I lit a cigarette with trembling hands.

In my relief, I'm afraid I paid little attention to the other questions of that round—I know the Padre stopped at two, having identified the opening words of *Treasure Island* and the closing sentence of *Finnegans Wake* (trust the Army Education Corps to give James Joyce a good airing), and McCaw picked up useful yardage over Lloyd George and the peerage. It was Forbes who really stole the show—either in emulation or out of sheer confidence he demanded a ten-pointer and was asked what sports he would expect to see at The Valley, Maple Leaf Gardens, Hurlingham, Hileah and—this was a vicious one—Delphi. He just cleared his throat, said "Way-ull", and then trotted them out:

"Fitba'—aye, soccer" (this with disdain for the effete

term), "ice hockey, ra polo, racin', in America, an' athletics—the Greeks in the auld days."

I applauded as hard as any one—frankly, while I knew Forbes was an authority, he'd shaken me with his fifth answer. I should have realised that the *Topical Times* and *Book of Sporting Facts* researchers cast their nets wide. (The Colonel was equally astonished, I imagine, over Hurlingham; you could see him thinking it was time Forbes was made a corporal.)

We finished the first round leading 26–15, and then the contest developed into a long, gruelling duel. I don't remember all that much of it accurately, but some memories and impressions remain. I know the Padre, after a nervous start, ran amuck through the Augustan writers and various artists of the Renaissance, with a particularly fine flourish over an equestrian statue of Gattemalatta, by Donatello, which had the Jocks chanting: "See the Padre, he's the kid!" Sergeant McCaw started no fires by attempting ten-point questions, but he was as solid as a rock on such diverse matters as the Jewish Disabilities Bill, the General Strike (I could hear the Padre mumbling snatches of prayer during this answer and trying not to catch the Colonel's eye), and the results of celebrated by-elections. He seldom failed to answer all three of his questions. Forbes was brilliant, but occasionally erratic; he shot for too many ten-pointers and came adrift as often as not, on one occasion even forgetting himself so far as to engage in a heated debate with Father Tuohy on whether gladiatorial games were or were not sport. ("Hoo the hell's a fella expected tae know whit a Roman boxin'-glove's called in Latin?") Nor, it was clear, would he have included the Emperor Commodus in his list of Great Heavyweights. I did reasonably well, but never equalled my opening effort. I tried one more ten-pointer, and crashed heavily over the Powers involved in the Pragmatic Sanction (really, I ask you), but scored a mild tactical success over the question-master by insisting that the victorious commander against the Armada was Effingham, not Drake. Father Tuohy backed me up (affecting not to hear the cry of "Your side got beat, onywye, padre" from some unidentified student of Elizabethan history in the audience), but the question-master hated me from that moment on.

We came to the half-way stage with a comfortable lead, and our Colonel produced a cigar from his sporran and sat back. He was anticipating, and not wisely, for in the second half we began to come adrift. The Fusiliers were finding their stride; two of them were only average, but the bespectacled genius of a warrant officer and the rotund major were really good. The major twice snapped up three-point questions on which I had failed (how was I to know the names of *all* the Valkyries), and on his own account displayed a knowledge of classical music and Impressionist painting which was almost indecent. I scrambled one ten-pointer by identifying five of the occupants of the stagecoach in the film of that name, and got a life-saving eight points from another ten-pointer by naming four of the Nine Worthies (God bless my MacDonald granny for keeping *Dr Brewer's Reader's Handbook* where my infant hands could get at it), but for the rest I was content to sit on my first two questions most of the time and take no chances. Forbes did well, with some fine work on baseball and the dimensions of football pitches, and McCaw continued his sound, stone-walling game, surviving one particularly blistering attack concerned with Gladstone's Midlothian campaign, and for good measure quoting "Keep your eye on Paisley", to the delight of the St Mirren supporters present.

The Padre was erratic. He pasted the Lake Poets all round the wicket, and caused some stir among the betting fraternity at the back of the hall by bagging two ten-pointers in succession (five trickily obscure quotations from modern poets, and a tour de force in which he identified five of the plays possibly attributable to Shakespeare outside the recognised canon. I can still hear that lilting Island voice saying slowly, "Aye, and then there wass *The Two Noble Kins-men*, aye . . ."). But he shocked the home support by confusing George Eliot with George Sand, and actually attributed an Aytoun quotation to Burns; it began to look as though he was over-trained, or in need of the trainer's sponge. And so we came to the final round, with a bare seven-point lead, and Father Tuohy announced that the last eight questions would decide the fate of the two-pound boxes of Turkish Delight which were the winners' prizes —to say nothing of the regimental honour and the Colonels' fivers.

We were proceeding in reverse order in this half of the contest, so that the sporting questions came first, and general knowledge last. I wondered if I dare caution Forbes not to try for a ten-pointer, decided not to, and sat trembling while he did just that. I needn't have worried: it was a football question, and he rattled off the names of forgotten Cup-winning teams without difficulty. And then his opposite number tried his first ten-pointer of the night, licking his lips and shredding a cigarette in his fingers, and as he identified obscure terms from croquet, backgammon, sailing, golf, and real tennis the Fusiliers' boot-stamping rose to a crescendo. We were still holding on to our seven-point margin.

McCaw looked awful. Normally pallid, he now appeared to have been distempered grey, but he folded his arms, gulped, went for three questions, got the first two, and then stumbled horribly over the third: "In American politics, what are the symbols of the two main parties?" He got the donkey, and then dried up. God forgive me, I toyed with the idea of doing elephant imitations, but my sporting instinct and a well-grounded fear that my trumpeting would not go undetected kept me silent. Still, he had got three points: our lead stood at ten. His opposite number blew up on his first question, and we came to the Padre's turn. His hands clamped on his knees below the table, he put up his head, sniffed apprehensively, tried to smile pleasantly at the question-master, and asked for the first of his three questions in a plaintive neigh.

"What," said the question-master, "are the books of the Pentateuch?"

It was, for the Padre, the easiest question he had had all night. They might as well have asked him his name. I relaxed momentarily—this was one certain point in the bag—and then to my utter horror heard him begin to babble out the books—of the Apocrypha.

We can all do it, of course—the sudden blank spot, the ridiculous confusion of names, the too-hasty reply. "Wrong," squeaked the question-master, and the Padre for once swore, and slapped his head, and cried "No, no, no!" softly to himself in sheer anguish. And we sat, feeling the chill rising, as the bespectacled warrant officer snapped up the Padre's question, got two points for it, conferred briefly with the stout major, and elected for the regulation three questions, which he answered perfectly for a total of another six. Our lead had been cut to a mere two points.

It was nasty. I looked across at the stout major, and he grinned at me, drumming his fingers on the table. I grinned back, sweating. The dilemma was—should I go for the regulation three questions, which at best might give me a total of six points? If I got the six, then his only hope would be a ten-point question; if I stumbled on any of my questions, he could have a shot at them for bonus points, and with his own questions still to come he could probably win the match. Again, he might fail one of his questions, and I would have a chance at it ...

Or should I try for ten? If I did, and got it, that was the game in the bag; if I came a cropper, he had only three points to make on his own questions for victory. I looked along at my companions; the Padre was sunk in gloom, but Forbes suddenly spread his ten fingers at me, scowling fiercely. McCaw nodded.

"Ten-pointer, please," I said, and the Jocks chanted encouragement, while the stout major smiled and nodded and called softly: "Good luck."

And then it came, in all its horror. "What were the names of the five seventeenth-century statesmen whose initials made up the word 'Cabal'?"

"Ca-what?" said a voice in the audience, and was loudly shushed.

I didn't know. That I was sure of. For a dreadful moment I found myself thinking of cabalistic signs— the zodiac—and I hate to think what I looked like as I stared dumbly at the question-master. A cornered baboon, probably. Think, you fool, I found myself muttering—and out of nowhere came one gleam of certain light—whatever the C in Cabal stood for, I knew it wasn't Clarendon.

That, you'll agree, was a big help—but at least it was a start. Charles II—Dutch Wars—broom at the mast— de Ruyter climbing a steeple in childhood—1066 and All That—"They'd never assassinate me, James, to put you on the throne"—Restoration drama—dirty jokes in *The Provoked Wife*—oh, God, why hadn't I paid attention in history classes?—oranges, Nell Gwynn, Chelsea Hospital, licentious libertines—Buckingham! It must be! Nervously, I ventured: "Buckingham?"

The question-master nodded. "One right."

And four to go—but three would get me a total of eight points, even if I didn't get the last name. I went for the two A's—Ask-something—no, Ash! Ashley! I gulped it out, and he nodded. The other A was as far away as ever, but a worm of memory was stirring—one of them was a Scotsman—Laurieston? Something like that, though. And then it came.

"Lauderdale?"

"Right. Two more."

I was buffaloed. I caught the major's eye; he was no longer smiling. One more would do—just one, and I was safe.

"I'll have to count you out, I'm afraid," said the question-master, and he began to intone "Five-four-three—", and the Fusiliers took it up, to be shushed angrily by their Colonel. The temptation to shout "Clarendon! And to hell with it!" was overpowering—Cla—Cl-something—oh, lord—

"Clifford!" I shrieked, all restraint gone, and the question-master snapped his fingers.

"Right. Four out of five gets you eight points. Bad luck with the fifth—it's Arlington."

I should have got that. It's the name of a private baths in the West End of Glasgow—if you can't remember that sort of thing, what can you remember?

Now it was for the Fusilier major. We were ten points up—he could just tie the match if he went for the big one, which of course he did, smiling in a rather frozen way, I thought.

"Good luck," I said, but he didn't need it. He identified the five Great Lakes without a tremor (pretty easy,

I thought, after my abomination, but that's the quiz business for you). And as the audience roared in frustration, Father Tuohy scratched his head and said, well, that was it. The match was drawn.

And then the babble broke out in the hall, with sundry crying for a tie-breaker to be played. Father Tuohy looked at the question-master, who spread his hands and looked at the top brass in the front row, and they looked at each other. The mob was beginning to chant "extra time!", and Father Tuohy said, well, he didn't know; the only people who were in no doubt were the seven other contestants and me. We were all busy shaking hands in relief and getting ready to pile for the exit and something long and cold. And then the brigadier, rot him, got up and addressed the question-master as the noise subsided.

"There seems to be a feeling that we ought to try to—ah—fight it out to a decision," he said. "Can't you set a few more questions to each side?"

The question-master, stout fellow, said his questions were exhausted, including the ten-pointers. They had been carefully balanced, he explained earnestly, and he wouldn't like to think up questions on the spur of the moment—not fair to either side, sir, really . . .

This didn't satisfy the audience. They began to chant and stamp in rhythm, and the brigadier smiled indulgently and asked the Colonels what did they think? Both of them obviously wanted only to let well alone, with honours even, rather than risk last-minute defeat, but they didn't dare say so, and sat pretending genial indifference in an uneasy way. We stood uncertainly on the platform, and then the brigadier, with the air of a happy Solomon—my heart sank at the satisfied glitter in his eye—said, well, since there was apparently a general desire to see a decision one way or another, he had an idea which he thought might meet with universal approval.

I've nothing against brigadiers, as a class, but they do seem to feel a sense of obligation to sort out the lower orders' problems for them. High military rank does this to people, of course, and they tend to wade in, flat-footed, and interfere under the impression that they are being helpful. Also, this brigadier was obviously bursting to cut the Gordian knot and win the plaudits of all. So we on the platform resumed our seats miserably, and he seized the back of a chair and unveiled his brain-child.

"What I'd like to propose," he said, meaning "What I intend to dictate"—"is that we should settle this absolutely splendid contest with one final question. It so happens that, listening to the perfectly splendid answers that we've heard—and I would like to take this opportunity of congratulating both teams on an admirable performance—a jolly good show, in fact—and I know their commanding officers must be delighted that they have so many . . . ah . . . clever . . . ah . . . knowledgeable, and . . . ah, yes, cultured intellects . . . in their battalions . . ."

The Fusilier major caught my eye, raising his brows wearily, and the Padre muttered "Get on with it, get on with it", while the brigadier navigated back to square one.

"As I was saying, listening to this . . . ah, display of talent, I couldn't help remembering a quiz question of which I heard many years ago, which always struck me as very ingenious and interesting, and I'm sure you'll all agree when you hear it."

I'd have been willing to lay odds against that, but the polite soldiery gave him a mild ovation, and on he went.

"My proposal is that I set this question to both sides,

and whichever can answer it should be declared the winner. All right?"

Of course it was all right; he was the brigadier. Ivan the Terrible might as well have asked the serfs if it was all right.

"Well, here it is then," went on this high-ranking buffoon, beaming at his own ingenuity. "It's a sporting question—" my heart leaped as I saw Forbes sit forward expectantly "—but I have to confess it is a *trick* question." He smiled impressively, keeping us waiting. "Now, here it is—and if anyone can answer it, I'm sure you'll agree his side *deserves* to win." There wasn't a sound in the hall as he went on, slowly and deliberately:

"In a game of association football, how is it possible for a player to score three successive goals—" he paused, and added the punch-line "—*without any other player touching the ball in between.*"

He smiled contentedly around at the stricken quiet which greeted this, said "Now", and waited. Immediately there was a babble of voices asking him to repeat it, and while he did I glanced along at Forbes. He was frowning in disbelief, as well he might, for the thing was patently impossible. I know the rules of football as well as the next man, and it just isn't on—when a goal is scored, the *other* side have to kick off, which involves another player. . . . I thought feverishly. Unless someone put through his own goal, and then took the kick-off— but even then, he had to pass to *someone*—you can't score direct from a kick-off. . . . It was beyond me, and I glanced apprehensively across at the Fusiliers. But they were plainly baffled, too.

"Well, now, come along." The brigadier was grinning with pure restrained triumph. "Surely we have some football enthusiasts . . ."

"Ye cannae do it." This was Forbes, outraged at what

he accounted a heretical question. "Ye're no' on." In the heat of the moment, he forgot all respect due to rank, glaring at the brigadier, and the brigadier let it pass, contentedly, and said:

"I will concede that it is highly unlikely. I doubt if it has ever happened in a game, or ever will. But under the rules it is theoretically possible. So."

It was one of *those* questions, like the 155 break at snooker—it never happens, but it could. Thunderous consultation was taking place in the audience, with what appeared to be a fight breaking out in Twelve Platoon—and then Forbes was claiming attention again, shaking his black-avised head in furious disbelief.

"It isnae in the rules of fitba'," he pronounced. "It's impossible. Ye cannae . . ."

"Is that a confession of defeat from your side?" asked the brigadier, with silken cunning, and I hurriedly said "No, no!" and gestured Forbes to sit down. He did, glowering, and I looked anxiously again at the Fusiliers, but the stout major was shrugging his shoulders.

"Come along, come along." The brigadier was enjoying himself thoroughly, confounding the rabble at their own game. And as the platform sat in stale-mated silence, he looked round. "Let's throw it open to the *supporters* of both sides, shall we? Anyone—from either battalion? You can win it for your side. All right?"

They sat, glowering at him in baffled silence—all except in Twelve Platoon's seats, where some huge upheaval was going on. To my astonishment I saw McAuslan, apparently trying to wrestle free from Fletcher, mouthing inaudibly, raising a grimy hand in the press.

"No one?" the brigadier was saying genially. "Well, now, that's—what? You wanted to say something?"

McAuslan was struggling up, ignoring Fletcher's

fierce command of "Siddoon, ye bluidy pudden! Whaddy *you* know?" He lurched past Fletcher into the aisle, his face contorted, and said in a gravelled whisper:

"Please, sur. Ah think . . . Ah think Ah know the answer, but."

From that moment the evening took on a dream-like quality as far as I was concerned. There he was, Darwin's discovery, in his usual disreputable condition, buttons undone, hair awry, shoe-laces trailing, and—I tried not to look—his bag of chips still clutched in one hand. Suddenly he must have realised where he was and what he was doing, for he paled beneath his grime—he was out there in the open, with everyone looking, facing Authority, and this was a situation which McAuslan normally avoided as the blindworm shuns the day. The Colonel had slewed round in his seat, and was staring at him as one on whom the doom has come—well, no one likes to see McAuslan step forth as a representative of his command—and the brigadier blinked in disbelief and started back, before recovering and exclaiming: "Excellent! Good show! Let's hear it!"

McAuslan closed his eyes and swayed, mouthing a little, as was his wont. I could only guess that a sudden blinding belief that he, McAuslan, was for once possessed of knowledge denied to lesser men had got him up on his feet, but he was visibly regretting it now. I had a momentary vision of him transformed, with golden curls around his battered brow, and satin small-clothes in place of his unspeakable khakis, standing on a little stool and being asked: "When did you last see your father?" And then reality returned, and the brigadier was saying kindly:

"Come forward a little, and speak up, so everyone can hear."

McAuslan did an obedient forward shamble, and

then the brigadier noticed the bag of chips, McAuslan noticed him noticing, and for a fearful moment I thought he was going to proffer the greasy mess and invite the brigadier to help himself. Instead, he hurriedly stuffed the bag inside his shirt, wiped his hands almost audibly on his thighs, and croaked:

"Weel, it's like this, see."

And we waited, breathless, for the Word.

"A fella—he's a centre-forward," said McAuslan, and stopped, terrified. But he rallied, and went on, in a raucous whisper: "He pits the ba' through his own goal. That's one, right?" The brigadier nodded. "Well, then, this same fella picks up the ba' and kicks off, frae the centre. But he disnae pass, see. No' fear. He belts the ba' doon the park, and chases after it, and a dirty big full-back ca's the pins frae him—"

"Tackles him foully," our Colonel put in hurriedly, out of ashen lips. The brigadier, intent on McAuslan's disquisition, nodded acknowledgement of the translation.

"So," McAuslan gestured dramatically. "Penalty! Oor boy grabs the ba'—naebody else has touched it, mind, since he kicked aff—pits it on the spot, an' lams it in. Two, right?"

"That's right!" exclaimed the brigadier. He seemed quite excited. "And then?"

"Aye, weel, then." McAuslan glanced round uneasily, realised yet again that all eyes were on him, swallowed horribly, scrabbled at his perspiring brow, and ploughed gamely on. "Soon as the goal's scored—the ref. whistles for hauf-time. An' when they come oot fur the second hauf, it's oor boy's turn tae kick aff, see, 'cos the ither side kicked aff at the start o' the game. So—he does the same thing again—batters it doon the park, gets the hems pit oan him again by the dirty big full-back—

"The same full-back fouls him yet again," translated the Colonel, his head bowed.

"That full-back wants sortin' oot," said someone. "Jist an animal."

"—and there's anither penalty," McAuslan gasped on, his eyes now closed, "an' oor boy shouts, 'Ma ba'', and takes it again and belts it—"

"You've got it!" cried the brigadier. "First-rate! Well done!" For a moment he looked as though he might grasp McAuslan's hand, but thought better of it. "Do you know, you're the only person I've ever heard answer that question, since it was first told to me, oh, thirty-five years ago, at Eton. Where did you hear it?"

McAuslan confessed that it hadn't been at Eton, but inna boozer onna Paurly Road in Gleska; he had heard it affa fella. The brigadier was astonished. Meanwhile, around them, the audience were demanding that the answer be repeated, while those who had understood it were vociferous in complaint that it was a daft question, it couldn't happen—not in a real game.

"I told you," said the brigadier knowingly, "that it was *most* unlikely. A hypothetical question, purely hypothetical, which our . . . ah . . . colleague here has answered most satisfactorily."

The assembly bayed their disapproval of this—you cannot take liberties with football where British soldiers are concerned, and they felt the brigadier's question was facetious, if not downright ridiculous. (Which it was, if you ask me.) There were those insubordinate enough to suggest, from the back of the hall, that it was the kind of question that would have appealed only to a brigadier or a McAuslan. But the brigadier's serenity was not to be disturbed; he awarded the laurel wreath, so to speak, to McAuslan, who was now quite overcome at his own temerity, and was shuffling uneasily like a baited bear in the presence of mastiffs. The brigadier then congratulated our Colonel, who was looking as though the House of Usher had fallen on him, and led the applause. There wasn't much, actually, as the mob was streaming for the exits in disgust.

On the platform I scooped up one of the boxes of Turkish Delight, and gave it to Forbes to pass on to McAuslan—after all, he had succeeded where the cream of two battalions' brains had failed, and presumably earned the Colonel a fiver. Forbes sniffed.

"Dam' funny fitba' matches they must hiv at Eton, right enough", was all he said, but I know he presented the prize to its rightful owner, for I chanced by Twelve Platoon's barrack-room later that night, just to make sure the lights were out, and heard things. I had been marvelling at the fact that McAuslan's memory, which normally couldn't hold much beyond his own name, had somehow retained the answer to a catch-question overheard in a public house. Of all the useless, irrelevant information—and then I thought of my own vast store of mental dross, and humbly put the matter out of my mind.

At which point, appropriately, there floated out of the darkened barrack-room window a familiar voice:

"See, Fletcher, Ah'm no sae dumb. No' me. Who answered the man's hypodermical question, hey? Wisnae you, oh no, an' wisnae Forbes, or Darkie—"

"Ach, sharrup braggin', McAuslan. It's aboot the only thing you ever kent in yer life—an' a dam' silly question, too. Here, gie's a bit o' yer Turkish Delight, ye gannet."

"Fat chance," observed Private McAuslan, munching with audible contentment. "Youse hivnae got the brains tae know tae pit it in yer mooth. Youse arenae intelleck-shull."

And every time I watch the keen young brain-workers

on television effortlessly fielding questions on French literature and microbiology and Etruscan art, I think to myself, yes, all very well, but let's hear you tell us how a footballer can score three goals in a match without anyone else touching the ball in between . . .

Parfit gentil knight, but

The last place you would have expected to hear Private McAuslan sing was the Colonel's office; it wasn't that sort of place, and McAuslan wasn't that sort of chorister. In fact, it was news to me that he sang at all. But I knew his voice too well to mistake the keening, raucous note that drifted in through the open green shutters on the warm North African air, and the effect was such that the Colonel, who had been discussing pistol-shooting with Bennet-Bruce, the Adjutant and myself, paused in mid-sentence to listen in disbelief.

"What the devil's that?" he demanded, and having stalked to the window like a dyspeptic Aubrey Smith, exclaimed: "Good God, it's that fellow McAuslan. Is he drunk?"

It seemed plausible. I couldn't imagine a sober McAuslan, who in addition to being the dirtiest soldier God ever made was also of a retiring disposition and terrified of authority, being so incautious as to play Blondel outside a building containing the Colonel, the R.S.M., and the provost staff. But there he was, shuffling along the back path, waking the echoes with a parody of "The Man Who Broke the Bank at Monte Carlo".

> "Ah wis walkin' doon the Garscube Road,
> Ah wis taken unawares;
> They wis shoutin' honey pears,
> Git up them spiral stairs!
> Oh-h-h come oot, come oot,
> They're sellin' fruit,
> They say—"

What they said was lost in the crash of a ground-floor shutter being thrust violently open, and the voice of the provost sergeant administering a scarifying rebuke. The song stopped abruptly, and the blackened sepulchre of D Company did a hasty shamble round the corner of the building to safety.

"Blast!" said the Colonel. "Why the blazes must McGarry be so officious? I wanted to hear the rest of it."

There was a pause, and the Adjutant coughed diffidently. "It goes . . . er, something like this, sir." And he continued, in recitatif, where McAuslan had left off:

> "They're selling fruit,
> They say that plums is—or are—good for the gums,
> And noo—now—they're selling green yins to the Fenians."

He paused, blushing, and the Colonel regarded him with something like awe.

"Where on earth did you learn that, Michael?"

The Adjutant said he had heard his batman singing it a good deal; you could see he was slightly uneasy about admitting acquaintance with the ribaldries of the barrack-room. But the Colonel, a keen student of battalion folk-lore, was all for it.

"Extraordinary, I thought I knew all the Jocks' songs, but that's a new one on me. What's it mean—you know, what's behind it?"

Adjutants are used to answering colonels' questions on virtually anything; really, it's what they are paid for.

"Well, sir," said Michael, "so far as I can judge it's about this chap who is walkin' doon—er, walking, on the Garscube Road, which is actually a street in the north-west part of Glasgow, close to Maryhill Barracks, where the H.L.I. have their depot—I did my primary training there, actually—"

"I know all about Maryhill Barracks," said the Colonel, testily. "Get on with it."

"Well, the chap was taken unawares, it seems, sir, by other people shouting, er, 'Honey pears', you see."

"And what in God's name are honey pears?"

"Well, actually," the Adjutant was beginning to flounder, when Bennet-Bruce put in:

"I think it's rhyming slang, sir, like 'apples and pears' for stairs. It's one of the Jocks' slogans."

"Ah," said the Colonel wisely. He knew, if anyone did, about those curious barbaric cries like "Way-ull" and "Oh-h, Sarah!" and "Sees-tu" which are the curious currency of the Scottish soldier's speech; they come, no one usually knows whence, and as often as not vanish as inexplicably. "Well, go on," he told the Adjutant.

"Well, sir, they also shout 'Get up the . . . the, er, them stairs.' You've heard them shouting it to each other, sir, I'm sure. Not just in our battalion; it's a catch-phrase on the wireless." Which, of course, it was, round about the end of the war.

"But the bit about the fruit?" inquired the Colonel. "What's that about green things for Fenians?"

The Adjutant was looking buffaloed, so I helped him out.

"It isn't really easy to explain, sir. Green is the Catholic colour—Celtic, and so on—and the implication is that Fenians—Catholics—will be eager to buy, er, green yins—green ones, green groceries, and so forth.

There are alternative endings to the song, like 'Cherries for the hairies'—"

"What's a hairy?"

"A girl, sir, in Glasgow. Pronounced herry. And I've heard 'Grapes for the Papes', too, sir."

"Pape means a Roman Catholic," said the Adjutant brightly, and the Colonel withered him with a look.

"I'm not entirely ignorant, Michael. It seems to me this song has decided religious overtones. Extraordinary. Is it intended to be provocative, I wonder?—I gather from the sporting news that Celtic aren't doing too well these days. However, this has nothing to do with pistol-shooting, gentlemen, fascinating though it may be. McAuslan's in your platoon, isn't he, Dand? Well, tell the brute to confine his singing to the canteen, or some-where where I don't have to listen to it."

Which was hardly fair, when you consider how eager he'd been to hear the rest of it, but colonels are like that. So are company commanders; Bennet-Bruce tore mild strips off me afterwards because it had been one of my Jocks who had disturbed the peace of the Colonel's sanctum. "You'll have to do something about that chap," he said. "It's bad enough that he goes absent about once a month and is, at a conservative estimate, the filthiest thing that ever put on uniform. We can't have him cater-wauling under H.Q. Company windows as well."

"I didn't create McAuslan," I protested. "I just got him wished on me—by you, I may point out."

"Haven't heard him singing before, at that," said Bennet-Bruce, skilfully changing the subject. "It's odd —I mean, he's a pretty morose specimen, isn't he? Any-way, chew him up a bit, will you?"

I didn't, of course. There's no point, with the Mc-Auslans of this world. And I wouldn't have given his vocalising another thought if I hadn't heard him at it again, in D Company ablutions, on the following day. This time it was "Don't fence me in", with what he supposed was an American accent. I addressed Private Forbes, who was sitting on his bed with some of the boys.

"Forbes," I said, "what's with McAuslan?"

"You mean, havin' a wash?"

"He's washing, you say? And singing. What's he got to be so happy about?"

Forbes and the boys grinned. "Search me, sir," said Forbes, and from the secret look on his face I knew something was going on. There's a curious military shorthand which exists, in a Jock's expression and tone of voice, and if you can read it, it's worth a dozen confidential reports. I wasn't expert, like the Colonel, who could limp through a barrack-room kit inspection, smiling under his brows, and tell you afterwards which men were anxious about something, and which were content, and which were plotting devilment. But I was getting to know my platoon a little.

"It's a rerr terr," observed Daft Bob Brown.

"McAuslan hivin' a bath," said Forbes.

"See the man wi' the padded shoulders," said Mc-Glinchey, and began to hum, "Cuddle up a little closer, baby mine", at which the boys chuckled and winked at each other.

"How's Mr Grant and Mr Mackenzie gettin' oan wi' the wee brammer frae the hospital?" asked Forbes irrelevantly, and seeing my look, added hastily: "Aw-right, sir, Ah'm no' lookin' at you! Ah'm no' lookin' at you! Jist askin'."

"Jist askin'," said Daft Bob.

"Whay-hay-hay-ull," murmured McGlinchey.

"No kiddin', those two ought tae be gettin' bromide in their tea," said Forbes.

"Nae haudin' them in."

"She's a wee stotter, though, sho she is."

They nudged each other and avoided my eye. Right, I thought, two can play at this game, so I observed casually:

"When was our last platoon route march—two weeks ago, wasn't it? I think we ought to have another in the next day or so. The long one, down to Fort Yarhuna, where the sand is. We can camp out overnight." I gave them my benign platoon commander's beam. "And sweep under your bed, Forbes, it's filthy. McGlinchey, I saw rifle oil on your small pack this morning; show it scrubbed at company office by five o'clock. Right, carry on."

This is known as panicking them; I left the barrack-room in the comforting knowledge that they were calling down curses on my head and each others'—Forbes's especially, for provoking discord with sly allusions. It was all trivial stuff, of course, but interesting in its way. What, I wondered, could McAuslan's taking a bath—a portent, admittedly—have to do with the romantic entanglements of Lieutenants Grant and Mackenzie? My platoon obviously knew, and were disposed to be merrily sly.

As to Grant and Mackenzie, there was no mystery. They were the leading contenders in the championship for Ellen Ramsey, a phenomenon who had arrived on the scene a few weeks previously. She was the daughter of the R.A.M.C. colonel who ran the local military hospital, and, in the descriptive phrase of Private Forbes, a wee brammer, or, if you prefer it, a stotter. To quote the Adjutant, she had the message for the chaps. She was about nineteen, and as beautiful as only an English girl can be, very blonde, very cool, and with a smile like a toothpaste advertisement. The sight of

her skipping across the tennis court in her white shorts
had moved even the second-in-command of the battalion, an aged bachelor who despised all women, to
bite through the stem of his pipe; even the Colonel
observed that she was a damned nice gel, unlike the
usual little floozies who distract my subalterns and
cause 'em to make fools of themselves. That was the
unusual thing about Ellen Ramsey; she wasn't just
beautiful, she was nice with it.

So thought every man in the garrison, with Grant and
Mackenzie well ahead of the field, and their rivalry, in
that enclosed society, was what Forbes would have
called "the talk o' the steamie", which means common
gossip. There was apparently no other competition—
there seldom is, where Highlanders are concerned. They
have a built-in advantage in the uniform, of course,
which seems to attract women like flies; even American
airmen, loaded with money and Hollywood glamour,
can't really compete. I think, too, there is possibly a
kind of barbaric magnetism about military Scotsmen—
"it is," as small, plump, bald and bespectacled Major
Bakie of Support Company used to say, "the wild beast
in us, the primitive, feral quality of the bens and glens
and things." He presumably knew, since he was married
with a large family.

In any event, Grant and Mackenzie competed hotly
for the favours of Ellen Ramsey, and the community
watched with mild interest.

Personally, I couldn't have cared less. I was a confirmed misogynist of about ten days' standing, as a
result of my trip to Malta with the battalion football
team. There, in the intervals of going frantic over the
team's performance and frustrating the villainies of
Lieutenant Samuels, R.N., who had tried to harness
their ability to his own money-mad schemes, I had

become impassioned of a pert brunette in the pay-master's department, who had given me over for a sergeant in the Pioneer Corps (a sergeant, and a pioneer at that). I had rebounded to a red-haired temptress named Gale something-or-other, who had drunk my Pimms No. 1s and eaten my dinners at Chez Jim's, and had then turned out to be engaged to a local civilian.

So I had brought my fractured heart and ego back to North Africa, a changed and bitter man. I was through with women—finished, you understand. I could view even Ellen Ramsey with a dispassionate and jaundiced eye, smiling cynically at the folly of those who danced attendance on her. She didn't interest me. Anyway, Mackenzie was two inches taller than I was, with the flaming red hair of his tribe, and an undoubted gift of charm, and Grant owned a Hudson Terraplane. So I didn't mind taking up snooker again.

But Ellen Ramsey's affairs were all a far cry from McAuslan taking a bath, or so I thought until I had occasion to visit the hospital a couple of days later to see one of my Jocks who was recovering from a broken leg. Mrs Ramsey, Ellen's mother, a chatty, fearfully-fearfully Army wife who was the hospital's unofficial almoner, invited me to stay for tea, and in the course of a non-stop recital of the difficulty of getting domestic help in North Africa and the handlessness of Arab women as hospital staff, she suddenly asked:

"By the way, I wonder if you know a soldier in your battalion—yes, he must be in your battalion, because he wears a kilt, and talks in that strange way—I can *never* understand it—yes, he's called McAllan, or Mc-Clossan—something like that?"

"Would it be McAuslan, perhaps?" I wondered.

She said, yes, it would be, such an *odd* man. That

clinched it; I admitted, cautiously, that I thought I had heard the name.

"We see a great deal of him here," she said. "At least, Ellen does. I'm not quite sure about him—he seems rather, well—rough, you know. Oh, quite harmless, I'm sure, but he hangs about, you know what I mean, in such a silent way, and he looks—well, rather uncouth. I don't mean to be unkind, because he's always perfectly civil, when he talks, which he seldom does—not to me, at least, but of course I hardly see him. He seems very interested in Ellen, but of course all young men are— we've grown used to that." She gave that whimsical, satisfied, fed-up smile. "But he is rather different—well, he is rather . . ." she hunted for a word and came out with a beauty—". . . shop-soiled, I think. Common, really."

Uncommon, was the way I'd have described Mc-Auslan, but for the rest I knew exactly what she meant. Having him about the premises was rather like playing host to Peking Man, until you got used to it. But her report was disturbing.

"Do you mean he annoys Ellen?" I asked.

"Oh, no—not at all. She rather likes him—and he was very good to her, really. Rather a knight-errant, in fact. You know that Ellen shops in the afternoons, down at the bazaar, for flowers and fruit and things for the patients? Well, on one of her first trips, a week or so ago, she went beyond the main market, down to the place they call the Old Suk, near the harbour—" I knew it, a rough quarter, and out of bounds to troops. "She tried to buy something from a stall—I forget what—and the proprietor, who seems to have been one of the more beastly Arab vendors, got unpleasant, and tried to bully her into buying at an exorbitant price. She wouldn't, of course, and then some of his friends collected, and one of them tried to get her wrist-watch, and it was all very horrid and frightening, as you can imagine, because of course she doesn't speak any Arabic, and there wasn't a white person about, and they were menacing her—you know what they can be like. Of course, she was a little idiot to go there unescorted, but she didn't know, you see."

I saw, and knowing what out-of-bounds markets in the Middle East can be like, I could guess that for a girl straight out from England it must have been a terrifying experience.

"Well, it was becoming really unpleasant, with these awful people pawing at her, and trying to snatch her shopping-bag, and laughing, and so forth, when suddenly this man McCollin—"

"McAuslan."

"—came on the scene. He asked her if she was all right, and she told him, and he turned on the biggest Arab, and told him in no uncertain terms to take himself off." That must have been something to hear, too. "But the Arabs wouldn't, at first, so he suddenly rushed at one of them, and knocked him down. That seemed to bring them to their senses, for they left Ellen and Mc-Allan alone, and he brought her back to the main shopping streets. She was badly shaken, poor child, and it was really awfully kind of him."

One up to you, McAuslan, I thought; that's your next offence scrubbed off before you've committed it. He could have got himself very badly beaten up, or even killed, mixing it with the kind of unlicensed victuallers who inhabited the Old Suk—where he had no business to be, of course, but that was by the way.

"And since then," Mrs Ramsey continued, "he seems to have appointed himself Ellen's unofficial bodyguard. She finds him waiting outside the hospital gates each afternoon, and he carries her basket, and I gather makes himself extremely useful in finding the best stalls and the cheapest prices. He seems to have a way with the Arab shopkeepers, you know what I mean? And afterwards he escorts her back again, carrying her parcels. My husband has nicknamed him 'Ellen's poodle', but I'm afraid he isn't what you would call house-trained. She asked him in for tea one afternoon—I gather he was extremely reluctant, and really she should have known better—and I was glad, I can tell you, that there was no one else on the verandah. It was rather embarrassing—well, I found it impossible to make out what he said, for one thing, and he seemed quite unaccustomed to afternoon tea, poor man. Yes, he is rather rough."

"Just as well, really," I found myself saying. "It has its uses, doesn't it?"

"You mean—oh, rescuing Ellen. Yes," she laughed a little doubtfully, "I suppose so. Oh, he seems to make himself useful, so I don't mind—as long as she doesn't invite him to our next cocktail party. That would be a little too much. You will be coming, Mr MacNeill, won't you?—Saturday, at seven."

"That's awfully kind of you," I said, "but I've a dreadful feeling I'm orderly officer this weekend. If I can't make it, please accept my apologies in advance."

I wasn't going to make it, which was petty, if you like, but somehow I suddenly felt I'd had just a trifle too much of Mrs Ramsey's hospitality—house-trained though I presumably was. Poor McAuslan—he wouldn't bat an eye when confronted with half a dozen Arabi thugs, but he must have been scared stiff in the presence of the gracious Mrs Ramsey and her best bone china. I thought of that scruffy, awkward figure glowering uncertainly at the thin brown bread and mumbling incoherently over his cup, and found I was cutting at the air with my walking-stick as I walked down the hospital drive.

Poor unseemly Glasgow Galahad. He had done a very proper, brave thing—gallant, if you like—and his eventual reward had been to feel uncomfortable and humiliated in the presence of the Colonel's lady—not that she could help being what she was any more than he could. And fairly obviously he had been sore smitten by Ellen Ramsey, which no private soldier of Mc-Auslan's social undesirability could afford to be—not even in the democratic aftermath of the Second World War. We are meant to pretend that social distinctions are a thing of the past, but as in all things it depends who are the individuals involved. Take McAuslan, and you might as well apply the conventions of the Middle Ages. You wouldn't want him hanging round your daughter, I'll tell you.

Still, I found myself disliking Mrs Ramsey's grande dame implications. And also regretting—as I'd often done—Private McAuslan's thick-headedness; why hadn't he just faded out gracefully, after doing his good deed? But he hadn't, and he didn't—the day after I had been at the hospital I happened to be driving down town to the Stadium, and saw Ellen Ramsey obviously coming back from her afternoon's shopping. She was sitting in one of those two-person horse-gharries, looking like the front row of the chorus, and who should be in the other seat, half-hidden under a load of parcels, but Old Man Karloff himself. He was grinning, in a bashful sort of way, and obviously as pleased as Punch —no wonder he had started taking baths and went about the place singing.

I wondered if I should do something about it. It seemed to me that McAuslan was liable to get himself hurt. But what to do? He was infringing no military rule; he wouldn't, poor soul, have understood what it was all about—neither, I think, would Ellen Ramsey. It was all so trivial and unimportant—but so are many potentially disastrous things, and they become disasters simply because, being trivial at the outset, you can't take hold of them.

Anyway, it all came to a head a few days later, in a way which, looking back, seems totally unreal. I went to Mrs Ramsey's cocktail party after all—well, it was free drink and liver on sticks, and I wasn't going to face the Saturday night cold meat in the mess with the prospect of being roped in to the second-in-command's bridge game afterwards. So I went to the hospital, where the garrison's finest were circulating and knocking back the gin; there were about thirty people on the Ramseys' verandah, making the usual deafening cocktail-party chatter, and I latched on to a glass and made heavy play among the cheese and grapes and wee biscuits with paste on them. In between I heard about adrenalin from old man Ramsey, his wife told me that she didn't know what she was going to do about the Arab hospital sweepers who were certainly pilfering from the stores not that she minded the loss so much as the fact that they would certainly contaminate the foodstuffs, the Padre from the Fusiliers wanted to know, in a round-about way, what provision was made for the spiritual nourishment of Anglicans in a Highland battalion, and the dockyard captain, plashing with gin, told me about his early training days on a windjammer. All the usual stuff, and then, having done my duty, I retired to a corner to chat up one of the nurses—you can't be a misogynist for ever.

It was then I noticed Ellen Ramsey. She was, as usual, between Mackenzie and Grant, but I noticed she kept glancing in my direction—well, poor butterfly, I thought, it was bound to happen sooner or later. And then she gave me an undoubted look, and I detached myself and went over to a quiet corner of the verandah. She slipped away from Mackenzie and Grant and came across.

"You're Dand MacNeill, aren't you?" she said, and I found myself reflecting comfortably that two centuries earlier some fair Venetian had probably said, "You're Giacomo Casanova, aren't you?" in just the same way. So I gave my nonchalant bow, and then she ruined the effect by saying,

"Yes, Jimmy said you were." Jimmy was Grant, the Terraplane-driver.

"Do you mind if I ask you something?" she went on. Frankly, I didn't; faced with something that looks like the young Lana Turner, I'm as impressionable as the next man.

"I'm probably being silly, but—well, I thought I ought to ask someone. Look—you're John McAuslan's platoon commander, aren't you?"

I hadn't expected that, at any rate—it was nearly as surprising as hearing someone use McAuslan's Christian name—bad platoon commander that I was, I'd never really thought of his having one. But the surprises hadn't really started.

"I know I'm being stupid," she said, looking embarrassed, "but I had a rather odd experience this afternoon. No, please don't laugh. It's just—well, he's been helping me quite regularly lately, down at the market, carrying parcels and that sort of thing, you know, being generally useful . . ."

"I know, your mother told me."

"Yes, well, then you know he helped me out with some beastly Arab—and he seemed very anxious to go on helping, and well, he *did* know his way around the market, you know . . ." She shrugged, and spilled some drink from her glass. "Oh, damn, sorry . . . but, well, he seemed all right, although he looked pretty awful—well, he does, doesn't he? And then . . . this afternoon . . ."

"What about this afternoon?" I asked, feeling all sorts of nameless dreads.

"Well, this afternoon—" she looked me in the eye "—he proposed to me."

For a moment I nearly laughed, and then, very quickly, I didn't want to. She wasn't even smiling—her pretty face was perplexed and unhappy. I was relieved, and astonished, and angry, and—no other word for it—fascinated.

"Let me get it right. McAuslan proposed to you—marriage?"

"Yes, on the way home. We usually come back by horse-carriage, and it was a nice afternoon, and I thought it would be nice to drive along the front, and look at the wrecks in the bay—and on the way . . . he asked me to marry him."

Oh, God, McAuslan, I thought. Think of the improbable, and he'll do it every time.

"I didn't really understand at first—you know he doesn't talk very much—well, he hasn't to me, at least. Just when we were in the market, and so on, and I don't understand a lot of it anyway—it's his accent. And when he started talking this afternoon, I couldn't make much of it out, and then it dawned on me . . . there wasn't any doubt of it. He was proposing."

"You're sure?" I was trying to hold on to reality. "What did he say, exactly?"

"Oh, gosh, I couldn't reproduce it." She was very much a schoolgirl, really. "But he said, 'We could get married'—merit, he called it. He said it again."

"You're sure . . . he wasn't being funny?"

"Oh, no. No. He was dead serious. I've been proposed to before—once—not half as seriously as he did. He meant it. It never even occurred to me to treat it as a joke." She looked uncertain, frowning. "I couldn't have."

"What did you say—I mean, if it's any of my business?"

"Well, when I'd got over the surprise, and realised he was being serious, I said—I said no. Look, honestly, I know this sounds terribly silly to you, and you probably think I'm an idiot, or that I think it's all a big giggle, or something, but I don't—really, I don't. I mean, if I had, I wouldn't have wanted to tell you, would I?"

"Well," I said. "Well—why are you . . . telling me?"

"Because I'm worried. All right, you probably think it's a great hoot, but it isn't. I said no, you see . . . and he asked me again, in that sort of dogged way, and I said, 'No, look, please, it isn't on. I mean, I don't want to get married.' And he asked me again, very seriously, and I said no, and tried to explain . . . and then—you won't believe this . . ."

"I'll believe anything," I said, and meant it.

"Well, he started to cry. He just looked at me, very steadily, and then tears started to run down his cheeks. Positive tears, I mean. He didn't sob, or anything like that. He just . . . well, wept. I asked him not to, but he just stared at me, and then he climbed out of the carriage, and walked away. I didn't know what to think. And then he came back, and looked at me, and said, 'It's no' bluidy fair.' That's what he said. And then he said, 'Good afternoon' and walked off. I mean, it's mad, isn't it?"

She stood smiling at me, with that puzzled look in her big, blue eyes, and I wondered for an instant if this was some fearful joke thought up by her and Messrs Mackenzie and Grant to take the mickey out of me. But it wasn't, and she was worried.

"Well," I said, "I don't know about mad—but it's certainly unexpected. I don't really know. . ."

"Look, I'm awfully sorry even mentioning it. . . I feel an awful fool . . . but . . . I mean he's really a terribly nice person—I think—but, well, it worries me. He can be pretty savage, you know—if you'd seen him with that Arab, I mean, just for a minute he was really berserk. I mean, he seemed pretty badly cut-up this afternoon—he really looked awful—more awful, I mean." She suddenly put down her glass. "Look, I don't think I'm a femme fatale, or anything, and I know it sounds like something out of *Red Letter*, but he wouldn't do anything silly, would he?"

The answer to that was yes, of course, he being Mc-Auslan, but whatever it was, it would be some folly no one had thought of yet.

"No," I said, "I shouldn't think so."

"Please, don't think I'm being stupid—well, I am, I suppose, getting all in a tizzy about nothing. Only I wanted to tell someone—and you're his platoon commander—and he said something about you once—not today—and well . . . I wouldn't want him to think that I was laughing at him, or anything like that. I mean most boys . . ." She gave a gesture that would have belted Grant and Mackenzie right in the ego ". . . you know how it is. But, he's so serious . . . he really is. It's really silly, isn't it? And I'm the genuine dumb blonde, aren't I?"

No, I thought, you're a rather nice girl; dumb, yes, in some ways, but nice with it.

"Well," I said, "you didn't laugh at him, so . . ."

"No," she said, "I didn't laugh."

"So that's all there is to it," I said.

"Look . . . maybe I shouldn't have said anything . . .
I mean, he won't get into any kind of trouble, will
he?"

"Why should he? Proposing isn't a crime."

"No, I suppose not . . . but if Daddy knew, he'd be
hopping mad. Mummy," she added elegantly, "would
bust a gut. And I hate to think what Jimmy Grant or
Iain would do about it."

"If either Lieutenant Grant or Lieutenant Mackenzie
were ill-advised enough to try to do anything about a
member of my platoon," I said, "you would be bringing
fruit and flowers for them in the afternoons."

"Good. Could you get me another punch, please? I
feel I need it after all this confessional stuff. Look, do
you think I'm barmy? It all sounds so dam' silly, doesn't
it?"

Take anyone's proposal of marriage, and the chances
are it will sound silly. Hollywood has overworked the
truth of how people talk to the extent that reality, when
you come across it, usually sounds corny. I remember a
fellow in Burma being shot in the leg, and he rolled
over shouting: "They got me! The dirty rats, they got
me!" Put that into fiction and people will laugh at it, but
I heard it happen.

Similarly, the remarkable conversation I had just had
with Ellen Ramsey. It was, as she said, damned silly,
but I knew it was true, and that to McAuslan it had
probably been a bit of a tragedy, and in no way funny.
The thought of her and McAuslan doing the Jane
Austen bit—and no doubt looking like something left
out for the cleansing department while he did it—
should, in theory, have been ludicrous. But she didn't
think so, and neither did I. It was pathetic, and rather
touching, and not for the first time I found myself un-

comfortably moved by that uncertain, unhappy, vulnerable little tatterdemalion. It must have hurt him, and I wondered how he was taking it.

It wasn't just a sentimental consideration, either. I knew my McAuslan; under the bludgeonings of fate, in whatever form, his normal reaction was to go absent, and I didn't want that. He had been over the wall too often in the past, and if he did it again he could be in serious trouble. So I took the precaution of checking the guardroom list that midnight, and sure enough, his name was among those who had failed to book in by 2359 hours.

Normally, when a man does that, you expect to see him returned within a few hours, full of flit and defiance, by the gestapo. But I decided to take no chances; I rang a friend in the provost marshal's office, one of the half-human ones, and asked him to do a quick sweep with his redcaps for one McAuslan, J., that well-known wanderer, and whip him back to barracks as fast as possible.

"I don't want him going A.W.O.L., Charlie," I explained. "His record won't stand it. Try the Old Suk; he's probably rolling in some gutter with a skinful of arak."

"It beats me why you want him back," said Charlie, "but leave it to me; my boys'll find him."

But they didn't. Sunday noon came, without result, and McAuslan's name went up on the board as absent without leave. That was bad enough; my next fear was that he had done something really daft, like hopping an outward-bound ship, in which case his absence would become desertion. He couldn't, I asked myself, do anything worse, could he? Jilted people are capable of anything, and I began to see visions of McAuslan à la Ophelia, floating belly-up with rosemary and fennel twined in his hair. It had got to the point where I was trying to translate "Adieu, cruel world" into Glasgow patter, when the mess phone rang.

"We got your lad," said Charlie. "Not in the Suk, not in Puggle Alley, not on the harbour—guess where? Out on the beach, looking at the wrecks, for God's sake. Talk about eccentrics."

"Thanks, Charlie. How is he?"

"Tight as a coot, but past the fighting stage—now. We had a little trouble. He should be arriving at your rest home any minute. O.K.?"

I thanked him and hung up, quite unreasonably relieved. Then after a few minutes I went round to the guardroom, and Sergeant McGarry admitted me to a cell to view the remains.

Even by McAuslan standards, his condition was deplorable. He had evidently got extremely wet, and thereafter spent the night on a well-nourished compost heap, his sporran and one boot were missing, his matted hair hung over a face that looked like a grey-washed cathedral gargoyle, and he had a new black eye. He was also three-parts drunk, and swayed to and fro on the edge of his plank-bed, making awful sounds.

Becoming aware of me he tried to focus, made an effort to get up, and wisely desisted.

"Ah'm—Ah'm awfy—sorry, sir," he said at last, articulating with difficulty.

"So am I," I said, and he groaned.

"Ah'm gaunae—gaunae be sick," he announced.

"Sergeant McGarry!" I shouted. "He's going to be sick. Get a bucket, or something—"

McGarry's face appeared at the grille in the cell door, scowling horribly.

"Spew on my floor, ye beast, and I'll tear the bones from your body."

"Ah'm no' gaunae be sick," McAuslan decided, and McGarry vanished. Psychologists take note.

I doubted if there was much to be accomplished in the prisoner's present condition, but you have to go through the motions. He would be before the Colonel in the morning, and if by previous inquiry you can discover some extenuating circumstance, or even coach the accused in what to say—or what not to say—it all helps.

"McAuslan," I said, "this is the fourth time this year. You'll be for detention, you realise that? Maybe in barracks, maybe in the glasshouse. You got fourteen days last time. You don't want to go to the Hill, do you?"

No reply. He was gargling to himself, staring down at his hands in a bemused way, giving occasional small hiccups. I didn't seem to be getting through.

"McAuslan, you were absent nearly a whole day. That's serious. How are you going to explain it to the Colonel?"

He looked vacantly at me, and began to mumble, at first incoherently, but then words began to come out. I don't know what I expected—I've heard guardroom depositions that you wouldn't believe, including a confession of murder, and poured-out grievances going back in harrowing detail to infancy—but none that astonished me more than McAuslan's. And yet, it was perhaps perfectly natural—but I'd never have heard it if he hadn't been deep in drink.

". . . no good enough," he muttered. "No' good enough. It's no' bluidy fair, so it's no'. Never done nuthin'." His eyes were unnaturally bright, but didn't seem to be seeing anything. "Ah'm—no' good enough. No' bluidy fair. Lot o' bluidy snobs. Thinkin' Ah'm jist a yahoo. Ah'm no'. Thought she wiz different, but, no' like the rest o' them bluidy snobs. See her mither, an' her sang-widges—bluidy awfy, they wiz." He gulped resoundingly. "Auld cow. No' good enough for her. Jist a yahoo. Sergeant Telfer says Ah'm jist a yahoo—a'body does. And her, she thinks Ah'm no' good enough. And Ah'm jist—jist . . ." He began to sob, deep in his chest, ". . . no' good enough. No' good enough."

I just stood listening; there was nothing else to do.

"Never got made lance-corporal—an' Boyle did, an' him's scruffy as—as—as me. Wisnae fair—wisnae my fault—no' bein' good enough. Ah didnae think she mindit, though—an' Ah sortit that wog oot, doon the bazaar. Ah did. 'You leave the lassie alone, ye black bastard,' Ah says, 'or Ah'll banjo ye. Git up tae me, son,' Ah says, 'ye'll git the heid oan ye.' That sortit him, right enough. Aye, but Grant an' Mackenzie an' them, bet ye they couldnae 'a sortit him. But they're good enough— toffee-nosed an' talkin' posh—good enough, aye. Ah'm no' good enough—Ah'm a yahoo—no' good enough. Sno' bluidy fair, so it's no'—no' bein' good enough!"

Maybe I'm soft, but I felt my eyes stinging. I squatted down in front of him as he rocked on the bench, working his hands between his knees. Self-pitying drunks are ten a penny, but what was coming out of him wasn't just ordinary self-pity. All right, he was abysmally stupid, and by exhibiting a phenomenal degree of wooden-headedness he had got himself hurt. So what do you do—tell him to get hold of himself and not be a fool? Perhaps. But when someone has spent a young life-time getting hurt, in ways which most of us can't imagine, then when he commits a really outstanding folly, and is reduced to utter abject misery, it may be as well to go easy.

"Of course you're good enough, son," I said, and presumably he heard, for he shook his head.

"Ah'm no' like Grant an' Mackenzie an' them. Bluidy

wee snobs—her an' her sang-widges. Thinkin' Ah'm jist a yahoo—Ah'll show them—Ah'm no' jist a yahoo—mebbe Ah didnae go tae a posh school, an' talk toffee-nosed, but Ah'll dae a'right. When Ah git oot, Ah'll dae a'right—there a fella in the Garngad—wi' a haulage business—gimme a job. Ah'll be fine, nae fear. Ah'll no' be oan the burroo—" that is, unemployed. "See Grant an' Mackenzie, but, bluidy wee toffee-noses, see them oan the burroo. Thinkin' Ah'm no' good enough. An' Ah'm no'! She disnae think Ah'm—Ah'm—good enough. Oh, Goad, Ah feel awfy! Oh, Goad, Ah'm awfy ill!"

He clutched himself and rolled around for a moment, but then steadied up, called on his Maker a few times, and observed fearfully that he was for the hammer the morn.

"Darkie'll nail me. He's a bastard, yon Darkie, so he is. He'll dae me. He's done me afore. They—they like daein' me!"

Since I *was* Darkie, this was slightly disturbing. It also suggested that McAuslan was well beyond the bounds of comprehension, so I decided to take my leave. I kicked on the door for Sergeant McGarry, and as he was opening up, I looked at McAuslan, crouched on his bench, sunk in dejection. It always comes as a shock when you see into someone's mind—it can be terribly corny, and trite, and obvious, and yet totally unexpected. It never seems quite real. It wasn't, I could agree with him, bloody fair.

"No' good enough," he muttered again, as the door closed.

The Colonel evidently agreed with him, for next morning he heaved the book at him—twenty-eight days' cells, which was the maximum he could do in the guard-room, without being sent to the military prison at Helio-polis. Sensibly, McAuslan took it without comment, beyond a mumbled apology, and that was that. He laboured, for the ostensible good of his soul and the damage of the battalion gardens, for his daily eight hours, and McGarry locked him up at night. I kept an eye on him, to see how he was bearing up, but beyond the fact that he got filthier by the day—which was absolutely normal—there was nothing to report. No signs of unhinged personality, or anything, although with him it was always difficult to tell. Whatever had been working in him that night, he seemed to have got over it.

It must have been in the last week of his sentence, and I was in company office late in the afternoon, when the battalion post clerk brought in the mail. It was a big batch, because there had been some mix-up at the air-port that had delayed things for several days; I sent for one man from each platoon to help sort it, splitting it into platoon bundles. The man from my platoon was Daft Bob Brown; he carried off a great heap of letters for his barrack-room, and as I was leaving the office I met him going down the company steps, a bundle of envelopes still in his hand.

"Where away with those?" I asked.

"Guardroom, sir. McAuslan's mail."

I was surprised. "He gets plenty, doesn't he?"

"No kiddin', sir. If it wisnae for him, postie wid be oot o' a job."

"But—" I said. "How's that? He can't read or write."

"That's right, sir. Ah write his letters for him—me an' the fellas."

"And read them, too—the one's he gets, I mean?"

"Aye, sure. It's a helluva job, too. Ye should see the amoont he gets—shake ye rigid."

"Well, I'm damned." This was intriguing. "Who writes to him—his people?"

Daft Bob guffawed. "No' on yer nelly. It's the birds."
"The birds?"
"The talent, the hairies, the glamouries." He took pity
on my ignorance. "The women."
"Women? You mean young women? Girls? Writing
to McAuslan?"
"No hauf. He's a helluva man for the lassies, yon."
"I don't believe it," I said. "Now, look, hold on.
Let's get it straight. You say that women write to
McAuslan—and he writes to *them*? Or rather, you and
the others write for him? What about, for heaven's
sake?"
"Oh, Goad, the passion," said he. "It's like somethin'
oot the *Sunday Post*, no kiddin'. 'Ah-love-ye, Ah-love-
ye, Ah'm-pinin'-away-fer-ye', a' the time. Me an' the
boys is hairless, keepin' up wi' it."
"Come off it, Brown," I said. "You're telling me that
McAuslan exchanges love letters with—with hordes of
women? Don't give me that—I mean, look at him. He
isn't Tyrone Power, is he? What woman in her right
mind—"
"Ach, they don't know ony better. Look, sir, ye know
the addresses that turns up in greatcoat pockets, frae
wee lassies that works in the packin' sheds in blighty?
Ye know, they pit their addresses in the pockets, so that
fellas that gits the coats'll write tae them? Some fellas
diz, but no' often. Weel, McAuslan collected a whole lot
o' these addresses, and gits us tae write tae the women
for him."
Freud, you should be living at this hour, I thought,
someone hath need of thee.
"What for?" I demanded.
"Ah dae ken. It's a good baur, though. He tells us whit
tae say—Goad, ye should see it. He's gaun tae mairry
them, an' tak' them tae his place on the Riviera when

he gets his demob, and Goad kens whit else. There's nae haudin' 'im in. An' they believe it, too."

"You're having me on, curse you," I said. "It isn't true."

"Ah'm no', sir, honest tae Goad. Ask Forbes, or Chick, or onybody."

"But—how long has this been going on?"

"Oh, months, sir. Och, it's jist a baur. Ah postit a couple for 'im the ither day—while he was on jankers. One tae a wumman in Fife, an' one tae Teeny Mitchell in Crosshill, an' one tae—"

"Stone me!" I exclaimed. "The—the—trifler! I could wring his unwashed neck! You mean he's pouring out his revolting heart to all these unsuspecting females—"

"Oh, he's daein' a' that. A right Don Joo-an."

"And I was sorry for him. No, nothing, Brown. All right, take our lousy Lothario his billet-doux, and just hint to him, gently, from me, that—oh, what's the use? Carry on."

I went on my way to the mess, reflecting with mixed feelings on Private McAuslan, demon lover extraordinary. I gave up; life is too short, really. And as I went up the mess steps, I found running through my head the words and music of:

> Ah wis walkin' doon the Garscube Road,
> Ah wis taken unawares—

Fly men

I had the Padre trapped and undone, helpless in my grasp; the rocks were about to fall and crush him. In fact, he was snookered, with the white jammed in behind the black on the bottom cushion, and pink masking the blue at the top end of the table. Also, he was twenty-five points behind.

Reluctant to admit defeat, as the Church of Scotland always is, he played for time. He stood there sweating and humming Crimond, a sure sign of his deep disturbance, fiddled with his cue, dropped the chalk, ran a finger behind his dog-collar, wondered irritably when the Mess Sergeant was going to announce dinner, and finally appealed for help to the M.O., who had been offering him gratuitous advice throughout the game but now, in the moment of crisis, had retired to the bar and was tying salmon-lures. (The M.O. did this habitually, carrying the tackle in his enormous pockets, and fiddling with bits of thread and feather at the slightest excuse.)

"Now Israel may say and that truly, we're stymied," said the Padre. "Lachlan, will you look at this situation. What's to be done?"

"Put up a prayer," said the M.O. irreverently, with

his mouth full of red worsted. He glanced at the table. "Left-hand side, a bit of deep screw, and come off three cushions." And then, just as the Padre has resigned himself and was preparing to attempt his own patent version of the massé shot, which in the past had necessitated heavy stitching in three different parts of the cloth, the M.O. added artlessly:

"Here, did you know that Karl Marx was related on his mother's side to the Duke of Argyll?"

"Is that so?" said the Padre, feigning interest and glad of any respite. "I never—"

"Lay off," I said firmly. I had been here before. When it came to gamesmanship the M.O. and Padre could make Stephen Potter look like a girl guide. I knew that the M.O.'s irrelevant interruption at a crucial stage of the game had been perfectly timed so that the Padre could delay his shot until dinner intervened, or I forgot the score, or a new war broke out, and I wasn't having it. I had been pursuing the Padre across the snooker table for weeks, and now I had him gaffed at last.

"Take your shot, you fugitive from the Iona Community," I said. "Play ball." And as he sighed and stooped over the table, remarking that there was no balm in Gilead, I added some gamesmanship of my own. "You're twenty-five behind, bishop, and dead, dead, dead."

"The poor soul, have some respect for his cloth," said the M.O., and it was at that moment, with the Padre poised on the lip of destruction, that the Adjutant came in to announce that we had smallpox in the battalion.

"Smallpox?"

The M.O. ran a hook into his thumb in his startled reaction, and swore luridly, the Padre's cue rattled on the floor, and I suspect I just stood and gaped. And then the Adjutant, who was normally a slightly flustered, feckless young man, given to babbling, took things in hand.

"Hunter, C Company, is in base hospital under observation. They suspect it's smallpox—"

"Suspect? Don't they know?" said the M.O., sucking his injured thumb.

"They're pretty certain. He's been vaccinated fairly recently, but apparently that's not infallible, right, doc? Okay, the Colonel's on his way in to barracks from his home, and the first thing is to get every Jock who is out of barracks back here, at once, for quarantine and new vaccination. You'll be at it all night, Lachlan, I'm afraid. You, Dand," he went on to me, "get over to the M.T. sheds, take every truck you can find, as many N.C.O.s as there are in barracks—I'll get someone to round 'em up—and go down town for the Jocks. Sweep them in, wherever they are—"

"It's Saturday night," I said. "They'll be spread half-way to Cairo . . ."

"I know that. At a rough guess eighty per cent of the battalion must be down there. You go through every club, canteen, dance-hall and gin-mill in the in-bounds area—I want them all, you understand. No stragglers, nobody overlooked. Start at the 'Blue Heaven' and send out foot patrols from there. Don't bother about the Suk, just yet. Just round them up, get them back here, tip 'em out at the gates, and back for another haul. Right—move!"

I was moving, fast, when the M.O., who was barking abuse down the phone at some unfortunate operator, turned and yelled after me:

"When were you last vaccinated?"

"Burma, '45," I said, disappearing. The M.O.'s motto was, if it moves, stick a needle in it, and if I was going to have a hectic night combing out the Jocks from an

Arab seaport which was more like a labyrinth than a town, I preferred to do it without a fresh load of his bugs coursing through my blood-stream.

"Take a wireless and op. with you," shouted the Adjutant. "I'll be in orderly room, taking signals."

"Roger!" I wasted one second putting my head in at the billiard-room door and telling the barman: "Don't let anyone move those balls—I want his heart's blood!" and then I was in flight for the M.T. sheds.

It would be nice to record that within two minutes I was humming down-town with a well-organised convoy behind me, but it never works out that way in the Army. I had to dig the M.T. sergeant out of the mess where he was playing darts, he had to start a hue and cry for drivers, some idiot had lost the key of the petrol store, the lead three-tonner wouldn't start ("C'mon, ye thrawn old bitch, cough for your feyther," the driver was saying as he perspired at the handle), the Adjutant's promised N.C.O.s were slow to materialise—and then Regimental Sergeant-Major Mackintosh appeared, armed with his nominal rolls, and looking like an Old Testament prophet who had just been having words with the Lord and getting the worst of it. But, as usual, everything flowed into place under his Olympian influence; N.C.O.s and drivers appeared, trucks started, headlights flashed on in the velvety African dusk, the M.T. sergeant roared "Embus!" and the R.S.M. addressed me gravely through my truck window.

"If I may advise, sir," said he, in that grave and heavy voice which he reserved for subalterns, rather like Polonius addressing a half-witted prince, "you might be best to stay doon the toon, supervisin' the collection of battalion personnel. I shall remain here to receive them." He paused, thinking. "I know you are aware, sir, that it is of the utmost importance that we bring back every wan of them. It may be difficult. There is a native population in the toon of an estimated wan hundred thousand souls—" (trust a Highland R.S.M. to say "souls", not people) "—so our men may be haard to find. Weel, just you stick at it, Mr MacNeill, and we'll get the job done, *namanahee.*"

Looking back, I realise that the R.S.M. was a desperately anxious man that night. Of course, he was an old and experienced soldier, and I know now that he was contemplating what an epidemic of that hideous disease might do to a battalion that had survived everything the Germans and Japanese could give it. Vaccinations, as the M.O. said, are not infallible. But I didn't really understand this at the time; I suppose I was young and callous and preoccupied with the job in hand. To tell the truth, I was rather excited, and slightly apprehensive on a different account.

As a subaltern, you get used to doing pretty well anything. In my brief time I had been called on to command a troop-train, change a baby's nappies, quell a riot of Arab nationalists, manage a football team, take an inventory of buried treasure, and partner a Mother Superior at clock-golf. This was in the days when the British Army was still spread all round the globe, acting as sentry, policeman, teacher, nurse and diplomat in the wake of the Second World War, and getting no thanks for it at all. It was a varied existence, and if I'd been ordered to redecorate the Sistine Chapel or deliver a sermon in Finnish, I'd hardly have blinked an eyelid before running to the R.S.M. pleading for assistance.

But descending on an Arab city on a Saturday night to round up 800 Scottish soldiers, many of whom would doubtless be well gone in liquor and ready to prove it, was a new one. Still, that was what I got my £9 a week for, so as instructed I descended on the "Blue Heaven," which was a cabaret-cum-canteen-cum-dance-hall just in-bounds from the prohibited Suk, or native market area. The "Heaven" was a well-known magnet for the more discerning revellers of the battalion, inasmuch as it provided local beer, Eurasian hostesses who danced with the troops and persuaded them to buy the champagne of the house (an unspeakable concoction known as "Desert Rose" in affectionate memory of the Eighth Army public conveniences), an energetic Arab orchestra, and two belly-dancers of grotesque proportions called Baby Boadicea and Big Aggie. If I could clear the clientele out of that on a Saturday night I would be doing well; I could despatch the foot-patrols to less raucous establishments like the Y.M.C.A. and the Church of Scotland Club to pry the patrons loose from their Horlicks and copies of *Life and Work*.

When we pulled up outside, the "Blue Heaven" was jumping like a geyser. The Arab musicians were administering extreme unction to "In the Mood", a glee-club of military amateurs was singing on the steps (they were bundled into the trucks before they knew it), and inside the establishment appeared to be on fire, so thick was the smoke. There seemed to be about two hundred tables, crowded with soldiers and airmen, all well-Brylcreemed and with their caps shoved under their shoulder-straps, the beer bar looked like the storming of the Bastille, and on a stage at the far end, Big Aggie, her brave vibrations each way free, as the poet says, was undulating with abandon, watched by an admiring circle of Jocks, arms folded, bonnets pulled down over their eyes, and mouths open in awe. Arbroath, you could almost hear them thinking, was never like this.

Calling the meeting to order was my immediate problem, made no easier by the fact that I was in civilian clothes. I shouted "Quiet!" at the top of my voice, without effect, seized a pint glass tankard, and hammered it on the table. Naturally it broke, leaving me with a splintered glass knuckle-duster, at the sight of which a battered Jock sitting nearby exclaimed "Name o' Goad!" and vanished beneath his table, advising his friends that I was a wild man and was going to claim them. For the rest, no one paid much attention, and I was left looking like a Broomielaw pub brawler in a Harris tweed jacket, which is a nice thought. Fortunately the M.T. sergeant took over, hammering a chair on the floor and roaring until the general din had subsided, Big Aggie stopped gyrating, and the Arab answer to Glenn Miller died away in an unmusical squawk.

"All right," I said loudly, divesting myself of my broken glass. "All Highlanders are to return to barracks at once. There are trucks outside. Fusiliers and other British troops, return to your own units as quickly as possible. Don't ask questions, don't waste time, don't wait to finish your drinks. Move—now."

This elicited the usual loyal response from the troops —a mutinous baying punctuated by cries of "Why don't you get a job?" and "Awa' hame, yer tea's oot." I knew enough not to stand waiting, but to get out and leave it to the M.T. sergeant and his minions to clear the place, which they did in ten minutes flat. As the crowd streamed out, snarling, puzzled, resentful or resigned, but at least obedient, I was buttonholed near the door by a small, perspiring Italian, who proved to be the proprietor, demanding to know why I was summarily closing his establishment, depriving himself and his numerous family of their livelihood, and assuring me that anyone who alleged he sold kif (which is hashish) to young soldiers was a liar. Nor did he water his beer, or run a bawdy-house, the hostesses being all cousins of his wife's on leave from their convent, and it was a vile calumny if anyone said his cigarettes were smuggled in from Tangier. Would I honour him by having a drink in his office?

I quieted him and went outside. It looked like the beach at Dunkirk, with Jocks piling into the trucks, drunks being lifted over the tailboards, the M.T. sergeant despatching the first of the foot patrols for stragglers, a fight or two breaking out here and there, and a Highland corporal arguing with two red-capped military policemen over the custody of a marvellously inebriated private who was lying prostrate on the bonnet of the M.P.'s jeep singing "Hand me down my walking cane" in a Glasgow accent. All in all, it was fairly normal, and no different probably from the usual chucking-out time at the "Blue Heaven"; most of them were going quietly, and I discovered why when a warrant-officer of the Fusiliers approached me and asked if it was right there had been a smallpox outbreak.

Since the murder was out, I told him yes, and to get his men home as fast as he could—and then a dreaded and remembered voice addressed me plaintively from the back of the first of our battalion trucks, which was fully loaded and ready to leave.

"Hi, Mr MacNeill! Hi! Sir! Here a minute. Ah'm no' hivin' this! You let me oot this truck, Michie, or Ah'll melt ye, so I wull!"

This was all I needed. I sighed and went over.

"What is it, McAuslan? Stand still and stop thrashing about. What's the matter?"

He emerged from the press of close-packed bodies, and clung to the tailboard, Old Pithecanthropus Erectus in person, even more grimy and dishevelled than usual by reason of his Saturday-night potations, and full of indignation.

"Here a bluidy liberty, sir," said he. At a rough guess, he was about six pints ahead. "Ah'm no' standin' fur it! Sharrup, Michie! Sir, they say Ah'm bein' took back tae barracks because Ah've got the poax."

"You've what?" I couldn't believe I'd heard aright.

"The poax. Ah hivnae got the poax. Dam' sure I hivnae. Ah'm no' like that. That's a bluidy awfu' thing tae say. Ah hivnae—"

"Oh, shut up!" I said, reasoning with him, and trying not to laugh. Trust McAuslan to get it wrong. "No one's saying you've got the . . . the pox, you silly oaf—"

"They are but! It's that Michie started it, an' Fletcher an' a', saying Ah've got the poax an'll hiv tae go tae the hospital, an' get pit on the V.D. list—"

Sober, McAuslan might or might not defend his personal reputation; flown with wine he invariably did, and in forceful terms. Knowing my man, I sought to reassure him.

"You've got it wrong, McAuslan. They're just kidding you. It's a smallpox scare—*small*pox, see, which is a different thing altogether—and much more serious. But you haven't got it, I'm quite sure." (It was tricky, considering McAuslan's permanently insanitary condition, guaranteeing that he hadn't got something or other—and then the chill thought struck me that he might yet catch it; we all might.)

"Anyway, everyone's got to go back to camp and into quarantine," I concluded. "And get vaccinated again. That's all there is to it."

"Aw." He digested this, the primitive features registering what passed with him for thought. "Zat right? Smallpox—no' the poax? Cos Ah hivnae got the poax. Ah hivnae. See, Michie, ye bluidy liar." Virtuously he went on, proclaiming his purity: "Ah been tae the M.O.'s lectures, and seen thae fillums aboot catchin' the clap an' that. An' Ah'm no' like that, sir, sure ye know Ah'm no'. An' Ah hivnae got the poax—"

"Aye, ye have," said an anonymous voice from the depths of the truck. "Ye've got everything, you. Ye're manky, McAuslan. Ye've got the bluidy plague. We'll a' catch it aff yez. . ."

I cut off McAuslan's impassioned denials, explained to him again that his associates were simply making game of him, told the rest of them to shut up, assured him that I personally had every confidence in his physical and spiritual hygiene, and was turning away when, just as the truck was revving up, a snatch of conversation from its cargo reached my ears over the Jocks' chatter.

"Hey, Toamie, ye hear aboot Karl Marx?"

"Who's he?"

"Groucho's brither."

"Away, he's no'."

"He's a bluidy Russian."

"How wid you know? Onywye, Karl Marx's feyther was a charge hand in a pub at Tollcross . . ."

The truck rolled away, no doubt with lofty debate about Karl Marx's parentage continuing (and Private McAuslan still loudly boasting his freedom from infection), and I pondered for a minute, as I watched the other trucks rumble past with their cargoes for quarantine, how these odd catch-phrases and slogans flew about Scottish battalions. Totally irrelevant, all of them. Only an hour earlier I had heard the M.O. mention Karl Marx, by way of persiflage, and now the Jocks had caught wind of it, and the great revolutionary's name would become part of their jargon for a space, a byword; there would be Karl Marx jokes, and he would be scribbled on walls, and fitted into marching-songs, and then he would vanish as suddenly from their culture, leaving a mystery, like Kilroy and Chad, for etymologists and philologists to theorise over—supposing they ever heard of it.

It took the best part of five hours to clear the town, with the trucks thundering to and fro, foot patrols beating up the bars and cafés and every conceivable haunt that might contain a Serviceman, Highland or otherwise, and a loud-speaker jeep touring the streets brassily ordering everyone back to barracks. The townsfolk themselves, who were used to the eccentricities of the British military, paid no attention; they lounged at the doorways of the Italian bars, or squatted on the street corners, or hurried past, like sheathed black shadows, in the direction of the Suk. I wondered if any of our fellows had strayed down there—it had only recently been placed out of bounds, as a result of nationalist agitation, culminating in a few outbreaks of rioting which had been dispersed by the local police, with the military standing by with fixed bayonets and empty magazines. Its only conceivable attraction at night-time (apart from the doubtful thrill of wandering in a genuine Arab city which hadn't changed much from the days of Dragut Reis and Kheyr-ed-Din Barbarossa) was the native bordellos, which were not widely patronised. Apart from the fact that we were a youngish battalion, and young soldiers in those days were far less addicted to brothel-creeping than their anxious elders supposed, it was recognised that the Suk could be a highly dangerous place. Besides, like McAuslan, they had been to the M.O.'s lectures.

By two o'clock the operation was virtually complete. I learned then over the signal set from battalion that the R.S.M. had accounted for all but about half a dozen

Jocks, and it was likely that the last foot-patrols would bring them in. From my point of view it had been a tedious rather than a troublesome business—indeed, the only real bother had occurred at the Salvation Army Reading Room, of all places, where one of our more studious privates, a graduate of St Andrews, had resented his ejection at the hands of one of Sergeant McGarry's provost corporals. As far as I could gather from a distraught Miss Partridge, the formidable spinster who ran the place, the root of the trouble had been the corporal's attitude towards reading in general, and this had somehow been taken by our private as a slight upon Goethe, whose works he had been studying. I wasn't clear how matters had developed, but expressions like "philistine" and "hun-loving bastard" had been bandied, and then the furniture had started to fly in earnest, the place being half-wrecked before the champion of German literature had been hauled off to the regimental sin-bin.

"It was a disgraceful scene," said Miss Partridge, "but really—what did we fight the war for? If one cannot carry the works of a distinguished author on one's shelves, foreigner though he be, without this sort of thing happening . . . well, it reminds one of the worst excesses of the Brownshirts."

I told her I doubted if freedom of publication had really been at issue, since I questioned whether the corporal's literary taste and prejudice rose much above the *Beano* and the Rangers football programme notes, but she said she would speak to the Padre about it.

I soothed her with apologies and promises that the battalion would clean up and make good any damage, advised her to go to the hospital for vaccination, and walked wearily back to the "Blue Heaven" and my temporary H.Q., which was the back of a 15-cwt truck containing my signal set.

The M.T. sergeant, who was holding the fort with about half a dozen Jocks, reported that the last foot-patrols had come in, bringing with them five Jocks who had been discovered in various holes and corners; he had despatched them to the battalion. I raised the Adjutant on the set, told him that seemed to be the lot, and could we now come home to bed.

He said "Hold on", there was muttered consultation audible through the crackling of the set, and then he came through again.

"Something's come up," he said. "We got your last five Jocks, but there are still two unaccounted for." More crackling. "Fagan and Hamilton—both C Company."

"Well, God knows where they are," I said. "We've been everywhere except the bottom of the bay. And the Suk, of course."

"Yes," he said, and there was a heavy pause. Then he went on: "Listen, Dand, it doesn't look too good. We've been checking around in the last hour, and those two are definite contacts—I mean they were in Hunter's company in the last forty-eight hours. Dand—you hearing me O.K.? They're contacts—we've got to get them back."

"I'm hearing you," I said. "Any suggestions where we should look?"

"Yes," he said, and through the static I could hear him taking a big breath. I knew then it was going to be bad news.

"Listen carefully," the crackling voice went on. "We think they're both A.W.O.L. In fact, we know Fagan is —he hasn't been seen since the day before last, when he was with Hunter in the Uaddan bar. Hamilton's been gone since noon yesterday—but he's a pal of Fagan's, so they may be together. And you know what Fagan's like."

I did; everyone did. A bad man from way back, with a crime sheet from here to Fort George. Not the same kind of bad man as Wee Wullie, whose peacetime service was one long drunken brawl but who was worth a hundred when the shot started flying, or the egregious Phimister of Support Company, who had gone absent almost weekly since his enlistment but had passed up the chance to escape from the Japanese at Singapore to let another man go in his place. Fagan was a real Ishmael, a slovenly, brutish, dishonest menace, a deserter in peace and war, whose conscription had been hailed with relief by the police of Glasgow's Marine Division. Since then he had been the regimental Public Enemy No. 1, and his periodic absences had been almost welcome.

But this time he might be carrying smallpox with him. I clamped the sweaty ear-piece to my head and listened.

"We've been digging around," went on the Adjutant. "We think he's in the Suk, and that he's maybe trying a home run."

"You mean, all the way to Blighty?"

"Yes. He's been borrowing money." The Adjutant's voice was beginning to crack with the strain of talking through the static. "Deserters have found ships before; the Colonel thinks Fagan's maybe on the same lark. We've got to stop him."

That went without saying. A smallpox carrier bound for Britain—the thought was enough to freeze the blood.

"But the Suk—" I was beginning.

"I know—but we think we know where he *might* be. You know the Astoria? Well, the rumour is it's the local equivalent of the Pioneer and Finlayson Green. You know what I mean.* It's just a chance, but it's all we've got. So it's worth trying, at any rate."

"You've been doing overtime on the intelligence work, haven't you?" I said, admiringly. "But look, Mike, isn't this a job for the redcaps?"

"No, it's not!" I started violently as the Colonel's voice rasped out of the earphones—the old villain had been listening in. "Official intervention in the Suk is *out* of the question in the present delicate state of affairs." He meant the trouble there had been with the nationalists, and he was probably right. But then came what was, for him, the real reason. "And I'm not turning the damned military police out for one of our people. MacNeill? Are you listening, MacNeill?"

"Yes, sir. I'm listening, sir. Sir."

"Right. Anyway, we don't know for certain that he's in this blasted brothel or whatever it is. But it's my guess, knowing the fellow's record, that he *is* deserting, and that that's where he'll be. If he's not, we've lost nothing by looking. If he is, I want him back. Got that?"

I said I had got it, and the Adjutant came on again.

"You've still got Keil—" (this was the M.T. sergeant) "—and some chaps? Good. Don't take more than four. Just a quick tool in, through the Astoria like a dose of salts, and out again—right? Nothing to it."

This is the kind of hearty instruction that turns subalterns' hair grey before their time. My guess was he'd be calling me "old boy" in a minute.

---

* The Pioneer was a legendary hotel in Bombay during the last war where, it was said, deserters from the forces in India could find a clandestine passage back to Britain, being smuggled out on homeward-bound ships. Finlayson Green is a pleasant, tree-shaded sward near the Singapore waterfront; it used to be said that if a deserter loitered there long enough, furtive little Chinese would appear and offer to arrange his passage to Australia.

"And don't, for God's sake, cause a diplomatic incident, old boy," he went on. "Just a quick tool in, all
right—"

"Yes, and out again," I said. "I know. Mike, this is
bloody dicey—"

"Piece of cake, laddie. Oh, one other thing—he may
be armed." I made egg-laying noises as he added almost
apologetically: "Seems he had a German Luger in his
kit-bag—you know what the Jocks are like for souvenirs
—well, it's gone."

"Oh, great," I said. "Sure he hasn't got an open razor
and a set of brass knuckles as well?"

"Knowing Fagan, he quite probably has. Look, take
it easy. There's a fair chance he isn't even there—in
which case we'll have to get the redcaps—" It was probably imagination, but I thought I heard a Colonel-like
snarl in the background. "Now, in you go. Good luck.
Anything else?"

I tried to think of something crushing, but couldn't.

"Did you know," I said, "that Karl Marx's ancestors
emigrated to Russia from Inverary?" I listened to his
anxious gabble of inquiry for a minute, and switched
off.

So, there we were. A possibly armed potential deserter
perhaps holed-up in a dive in a sensitive native quarter.
The diversions the Army can think up for its junior
officers are nobody's business. It's like a mixture of running an asylum and being a trigger-man for Al Capone.

I called up Keil and his worthies, and we conferred
by the tailboard. The street was very quiet now—it was
almost 3 a.m.—but there was a good moon, which would
be handy in the unlit Suk.

"Anyone know the Astoria?" I asked, and after an
embarrassed pause one of the Jocks reluctantly admitted that he did.

"Right, you're with me. And you two, and you, Sergeant Keil." I told them quickly what the operation was, and I'd have sworn that they looked pleased as they listened. Anything for a tear, as they say in Glasgow. They looked handy men—but suddenly I wished they were my own platoon Jocks—the massive Wee Wullie, the saturnine Fletcher and the wicked Forbes— yes, even the great unwashed McAuslan, who could, in his own words, "take a lend o' anybody—and his big brother". Not, when I thought about it, that we were likely to run into violent trouble—I hoped.

The Suk began at the old city wall, only a hundred yards from the "Blue Heaven", and once through the massive stone gateway you were in another world. Twisting, unpaved streets, black and shuttered houses jammed crazily against each other, with occasionally a light filtering through an ornately-latticed window or from a dimly-lit doorway; shadowy figures standing back under overhangs or moving in the dark alleys on either side—it was just like Pepe le Moko's Casbah, complete with romantic Middle Eastern night sounds, like:

"Whaur ye goin', Jock? Looking for bonnie lassie, yes? Come on in—hey, mac, where's your kilt?" And chants anent Auntie Mary and her canary. If you doubt this, you should know that the Arab is possibly the best imitator of the Scottish accent in either hemisphere, and loves to air his knowledge of the patois. So far from making a silent, unseen foray into the Suk, we were followed with interest by commentators on either side, and invitations from blessed damozels leaning out of the second-storey windows. I plodded grimly on, while the Jocks replied in kind, and presently we finished up in front of the neighbourhood's three-star caravanserai, a substantial building in mouldering stucco with

"Astoria" across the top of its peeling porch, a well-closed front door, piles of garbage out in front, and an admiring crowd watching us from either end of the street. There were lights in some of the windows, showing through dirty curtains, and the whole place looked as attractive as a disused gypsy caravan.

I confess I wondered what course of action to take. By rights I should have sent a man to guard the back door, but such was the town planning of the Suk that this would probably have entailed a walk of half a mile and then getting lost. I looked at the massive front door. Humphrey Bogart, who must have been in this situation dozens of times, would just have sidled in, somehow, shot a couple of hoods, seized a smouldering-eyed beauty by the wrist to make her drop her dagger, laughed mirthlessly, browbeaten Sydney Greenstreet, and then taken Fagan in an arm-lock and bundled him out to a waiting taxi. However, there were no taxis in the Suk, so I just knocked on the door. It seemed the obvious thing to do.

If no one had answered, frankly I'd have been at a loss, but presently the door opened, a vague female shape appeared in a very tight blue dress, a slim hand holding an unlit cigarette emerged from the shadows, and a husky voice said:

"'Allo, dolleeng—gotta light?"

I hadn't, as it happened, so I just said: "Good evening", and as near as a toucher added: "I wonder, do you happen to have a Mr Fagan staying in the hotel?" But fortunately, just as she was saying: "C'mon een, Jock—breeng you' friends", Sergeant Keil, a highly practical man, decided to take a hand. Where he came from, you didn't loiter outside a potentially hostile front door, in case the occupants dropped a sewing-machine on you from an upper window. He was past me and into the

dingy hallway before I could carry the courtesies any
further. The female shape squealed and disappeared,
the three Jocks surged in after Keil, more or less bearing
me with them, and my education in ferreting out
deserters began from that moment.

What you actually do is go up the stairs three at a
time, flinging open every door you come to, and waking
the dead with your shouting. If the inmates show resentment, you pass on, leaving the door open, whereupon
they come out to express their indignation, and your
associates, following some distance behind, can identify
them and see they're not the men you're after. There
were, in fact, four rooms on each of the Astoria's three
floors, and I wouldn't have believed you could get so
many Arabs, lascars, Negroes and their assorted ladies
into twelve apartments without everyone suffocating.
Within sixty seconds of Keil's eruption through the front
door, there was a milling mass of multi-coloured
humanity, in various stages of undress from full jellabah
and boots to complete nudity, on the first two landings.
I was struggling upwards past a grossly overweight lady
who, I think, was Italian, and shrieking to wake the
dead—and one of the deserters, Private Hamilton, was
emerging from a doorway on the third floor, his mouth
wide with fright, and then doubling back towards his
room.

Keil got him by the ankle, they thrashed about in the
doorway, and one of the other Jocks hauled Hamilton
upright and jammed him against the wall. He was naked
except for a pair of khaki slacks, and his first words were
those of the Glasgow keelie trapped and helpless:

"Don't hit me, mister!"

"Where's Fagan?" snapped Keil, just as I got free of
Madame Butterfly and about eleven small brown children who were darting about the stairway like tadpoles,

and came pounding up to the top floor. Behind and below me it sounded like the sinking of the *Titanic*; there were pursuing feet, but as I reached the landing the largest of Keil's Jocks slipped past me on to the top step, effectively barring the way up.

"Where's Fagan?" Keil was shouting again, and as his fist drew back the cornered Hamilton said:

"Eh? Eh?" and jerked his head towards the closed doorway next to his own. Keil threw himself at it, but it was too stout for him. He thumped the panels, shouting:

"Fagan! Ye've had it! Come oot!"

I glanced down over the rickety banister. In the dim light of the stairwell two rings of faces, one at each landing, were staring up—every colour from white to jet black, mouths open, frightened, bewildered, angry, and, above all, vocal. My Italian woman seemed to be dying on a permanent Top C, a large brown man with woolly silver hair was shouting and shaking his fist, and the rest of them were just generally joining in. I began to feel decidedly uncomfortable—not that they looked terribly dangerous, but it seemed to me our unorthodox entry into the Hotel Astoria was going to cause some stir in the neighbourhood generally, with possible ensuing diplomatic complications. But curiously, my chief emotion was a feeling rather like shame—at having roused and terrified so many ordinary citizens, and created bedlam in their hotel. It seemed a bit much— and then I remembered Fagan was a deserter possibly carrying smallpox.

Keil and another Jock were trying to burst in the door, still without success. Hamilton, released now, was standing pale and petrified; he was a gangly, freckled youth with a weak face and sandy hair.

"Hamilton," I said. "Fagan's in there—anyone with him?"

He licked his lips. "A bint."

I motioned Keil away from the door, put my head to the panels and called: "Fagan!" No reply. I tried again, and this time there was the clatter of something being over-turned, and a female squeal, instantly hushed.

"Fagan," I called again. "This is Lieutenant MacNeill, of D Company. Come on out and give yourself up."

This time there was silence, and while I stood listening Keil darted into the doorway of Hamilton's room, and came back to report that from the window he could see there was a roof adjoining the back of the building—a possible means of escape from Fagan's room.

"Fagan," I tried again. "Listen to me. You can't get away—we've got men all round the hotel. Now, listen. One of your friends, Hunter, is in hospital with smallpox. You were with him two days ago—that means you may be carrying it. You've got to get vaccinated, quickly —or you may get it yourself and spread it all over. D'you understand, Fagan? This is serious, man!"

There was a thin, wailing sound from inside, and a man's voice cursing, more clattering and rustling. I banged on the door, and suddenly his voice sounded:

"Gerraway or I'll blow yer —— head aff!"

"Oh, don't be a damned fool! You've had it, man! You've only been absent two days—what are you worrying about? But if you resist arrest, and try to get away when you're a smallpox carrier, you'll go inside forever. For God's sake man—" and it sounded terribly melodramatic, but it was true "—you can't go spreading a deadly disease about among innocent people. Come on —open the door! Fagan! D'you hear?"

There followed a couple of minutes' silence from the room—more than compensated for by the Pilgrim's

Chorus on the stairs—and then I thought I heard sounds of movement again.

"Fagan?"

Feet sounded on the other side of the door, and his voice came through the panels:

"MacNeill?"

"Yes."

A pause, and then: "Hunter's got smallpox?"

"That's right."

"Is that —— true?"

"Yes."

"D'ye swear that?"

At first I wasn't sure what he'd said; it was an unexpected question. But it was no time for quibbles. I said yes.

There was the sound of a key turning, and then the door opened. Like Hamilton, he was wearing only khaki slacks, a big, sallow, narrow-featured man with thick hair on his chest and shoulders. His hands were empty.

I motioned him out, and glanced into the room. There was no light, but the moon showed that the window had been thrown up, a jacket was lying over the sill, and crouched down beside the bed, on one knee, was an Arab girl—maybe not Arab, probably half-caste, wearing only a white petticoat. I had an impression of long black hair and big eyes staring fearfully; she looked about fifteen.

"Where's the Luger?" I said to Fagan, and he just stared at me. I reflected that it had probably been tossed far out of the window before he opened the door.

"All right," I said to Keil. "Take them down and back to the truck."

"Wai' a minute," Fagan said. He looked at me. "This

sma'-pox. Ah've been ——in' vaccinated." He jerked his head towards the doorway; the girl was inside still, making tiny whimpering sounds. "She hisnae. Ye'll get her ——in' vaccinated."

I daresay it shouldn't have startled me, but it did. Likewise Sergeant Keil, and with an N.C.O.'s suspicious mind he demanded:

"Whit the hell you on, Fagan?"

Fagan stared at him, and said deliberately: "Ah'll be lookin' for you one o' these days, china." Then he turned back to me. "Ye'll see she gets vaccinated?"

I didn't suppose that the local native authorities would even think of trying to vaccinate the population of the Suk; twenty to thirty thousand is a lot of people, especially when they don't much hold with Western medicine. Fagan wanted to make sure for her.

"I'll see she gets it," I said.

He kept staring at me a moment. "Right?" he said.

"Right," I said.

He went downstairs without another word.

Our strategic withdrawal from the top floor of the Hotel Astoria was a fairly fraught business; for a while I didn't think we were going to make it. Keil, with Fagan and Hamilton escorted by two of the Jocks, made it easily enough, simply by snarling menacingly as he descended and offering to murder anyone who got in his way. But my own exit was complicated by the fact that I'd promised to take Fagan's bint along; she screamed and wept and tried to hide under the bed until the remaining Jock lost his temper, slapped her soundly, and took her over his shoulder in a fireman's lift. We set off down, myself leading, and by this time the manager had appeared at the head of the excited multitude on the lower landings. At least, I imagine he was the manager

—he was a six-foot Soudani-looking gentleman, with
tribal cuts across his cheeks, a tarboosh on his head,
and a British Army greatcoat. He was also carrying a
club, and he affected to believe that, apart from disturbing the peace of his hostelry and forcing entry, I was
intent on kidnapping one of his guests for immoral
purposes. "Scotch bastard!" was the chorus of his complaint, in which the assembly joined with a will. Fortunately two native constables arrived, a discussion ensued,
and when I could get a word in—and that word was
"smallpox"—the more or less European element gave
one great wail and fled. We inched our way out, the
manager demanding to know who was going to pay for
Messrs Fagan and Hamilton's penthouse accommoda-
tion, so I gave him ten lire, at which he beamed alarm-
ingly and asked me to stay the night with his sister.
Honestly, I reflected as we hurried back to the truck,
I'd have been better working hard at school and getting
into university instead of letting the Army get its hooks
on me.

We dropped the girl off at the hospital, and really the
most painful part of the whole night was watching the
poor soul's hysterical submission to the vaccination
administered by a medical orderly. For some reason I
felt I owed it to Fagan to see the job actually done—
I hadn't worked it out, but I had a feeling that if it
hadn't been for her, he'd have been over the rooftops
and far away by now. Anyway, the nurses took charge
of her, I made my last call over the set to the battalion,
learned that Hamilton and Fagan were in safe hands
and every Jock was now accounted for, and that I could
go to bed. It was after four, and the dark blue sky was
bright orange at its eastern edge when I dismissed the
truck at the barrack gates.

There were lights on in the H.Q. building and one or

two of the barrack-blocks, but I was too bone-weary to go across. All I wanted was a long cold beer and bed, so I went to the deserted mess, got a bottle from the ice-box, and drank it in the empty, musty billiard-room. The balls on the table lay as we had left them; I stood smoking and studying them tiredly and finally rolled them into the pockets—the Padre's infernal luck would have got him out of the snooker, anyway; it always did. Heaven knows how they put in their time at theological faculties, I thought, as I slumped into an armchair, and the next thing I knew the Adjutant was shaking me awake, the sun was streaming in through the shutters, and the waiters were clattering crockery in the dining-room across the hall.

The Adjutant was as offensively bright as an advertisement for liver salts, throwing open shutters and singing to himself.

"Eggs and b. coming up in a moment," he cried. "Good old egg and b. Haven't you been to bed, you foolish subaltern? Drowning your sorrows in drink," he went on, picking up my fallen beer-glass from the floor, "or just sleeping off the great anti-climax."

"Wrap up," I growled. "What anti-climax?"

"Didn't someone tell you—oh, probably not, we didn't hear until an hour ago, while you were sunk here in your hoggish state of alcoholism. Ramsey phoned from base hospital—Hunter hasn't got smallpox. Nothing like it. Septic prickly heat, apparently, and not very extensive at that, but it seems some young doctor panicked and sent the balloon up, ringing the alarum bells and crying 'Blow, wind, come wrack'—and since by one of those damnable coincidences all the senior staff were out of town, well . . . we had a great smallpox drama for nothing."

He giggled, idiotically if you ask me (but then, an

effervescent Adjutant was the last thing I needed in the early morning), and went on:

"The M.O. went berserk, of course, when he heard—he'd been at it all night, up to his knees in lymph and lancets, using miles of sticking-plaster, and the entire battalion has got sore arms for nothing. Dammit," he added, "I believe I'm starting to itch myself."

"And serves you right!" I snarled. "While I've been tangling with armed deserters, earning a reputation as a white slaver, and getting mobbed by angry wogs—oh, and Miss Partridge is raising hell because the Jocks bust up her reading-room. I hope you enjoy dealing with her."

"Well, at least we've got Fagan in the coop," said he. "The Colonel's very pleased about that—thinks you handled it admirably. Come on, eggs and b., toast, coffee and all good things—"

"Oh, you go and get raffled, Michael Adjutant," I said. "I'm going to bed."

And that should have been the end of it, but there was a curious appendix. When I got up, after lunch, my orderly loafed in, on the pretext of cleaning up the room, but actually to convey the latest scandal and get my reaction. He pottered about handlessly, as usual, knocking my personal effects around, and after several irrelevant comments about the weather, observed:

"You're a right fly man, you."

I said "Eh?" intelligently, and he added: "They say Fagan's doin' his nut in the cooler. Haw!"

I didn't get the drift of this, so I told him to stop destroying the furniture and explain.

"Fagan's up tae high doh," said he, from which I gathered that Fagan was extremely annoyed and disturbed. "He says—or the boys say—you spun him a tale aboot Hunter hivin' smallpox, and Hunter didnae hiv smallpox at a'. An' Fagan's sayin' yer a bluidy leear—Ah mean, that you kidded him into givin' hisself up. That's whit the boys say—right fly man, you."

"Hold on!" I protested. "This is drivel! I thought Hunter *did* have smallpox—everyone did. Heavens above, d'you think I'd have been tearing through the Suk like a man demented, looking for one piddling little deserter—well, two, if you count Hamilton—if we hadn't thought there was a risk of epidemic? Come away, McClusky! We didn't realise it wasn't small-pox until—when? About seven this morning, I sup-pose."

"That a fact?" he said. "No kiddin'." And until you have heard a Glaswegian use these expressions you don't know anything about scepticism and amused dis-belief. "Aye, weel." He continued to potter, grinning secretly to himself. "That's whit the boys are sayin'— that ye kidded Fagan intae the cooler. No' bad. Serve 'im right. Naebody likes him. But he's in a hell of a sweat about it—says he's gaunae claim ye when he gets the chance."

"Fagan," I said, "can think what he likes. I couldn't care less. But I did *not* lie to him to get him to give himself up. You can tell him that, if you like, and add that he isn't worth it, anyway, and—"

"Okay, okay, sir," he said. "Ah'm just sayin' whit the boys are sayin'. Keep the heid—sir? Sno' ma fault. Right?" He shook his head, still grinning, as he stirred the contents of my wardrobe thoughtfully. "Right fly man ye are, though, so ye are."

The trouble was, he said it admiringly. Obviously the garbled tale would be all over the battalion about how the Macchiavellian MacNeill had conned Fagan into giving himself up by lies and false pretences. And I was still young enough to resent that fact—I didn't want to be thought of as a "fly man", whatever status that might confer in the Jocks' curious scale of ethics.

I told the Colonel about it when I went over to the mess, where he was lingering over his after-lunch whisky with the Adjutant, and he just roared with laughter, like the wicked old man he was. Then he regarded me from beneath his bushy brows, and re- marked:

"I don't know how long it took me—about twenty years, I'd say—yes, it would be in Ahmedabad, probably about '33 or '34—before the Jocks started to call me a 'fly man'. Quite mistakenly, I assure you. You've managed it in about six months—very good going in- deed." He gave me his quizzical grin. "You probably *are* a fly man, young Dand. Shouldn't be surprised if the Jocks are right."

"Well, sir, they're dead wrong if they think I spun Fagan—"

"Of course they are. In this instance. Don't take it to heart, boy. This isn't the Fifth Form at St Dominics; it's a battalion of Scottish Highlanders—heavens, I'm tell- ing *you*! You *are* one. They value all sorts of things— the usual military virtues and so on—but most of all, they tend to respect what the uncharitable would call craft. Like the Italians in that, I suppose. If they choose to think you're a fly man, just be thankful—however unearned you may feel the reputation is. You'll be sur- prised how useful it is." He smiled under his moustache. "If your night's frolicking in the Suk has taught you that, all the better. You can't learn too much."

"That reminds me," said the Adjutant. "I learned something last night—nothing of consequence, really, but it was quite new to me. Did you know, sir," he said to the Colonel, "that Karl Marx's grandmother was a Campbell?"

The Colonel raised an eyebrow. "No," he said, with mild interest, "I didn't know that." He thought about it a moment, and sniffed. "Mind you, I can't say I'm in the least surprised."

McAuslan
in the
rough

My tough granny—the Presbyterian MacDonald one, not the pagan one from Islay—taught me about golf when I was very young. Her instruction was entirely different from that imparted by my father, who was a scratch player, gold medallist and all, with a swing like de Vicenzo; he showed me how to make shots, and place my feet, and keep calm in the face of an eighteen-inch putt on a downhill green with the wind in my face and the match hanging on it. But my granny taught me something much more mysterious.

Her attitude to the game was much like her attitude to religion; you achieved grace by sticking exactly to the letter of the law, by never giving up, and by occasional prayer. You replaced your divots, you carried your own clubs, and you treated your opponent as if he was a Campbell, and an armed one at that. I can see her now, advanced in years, with her white hair clustered under her black bonnet, and the wind whipping the long skirt round her ankles, lashing her drives into the gale; if they landed on the fairway she said "Aye", and if they finished in the rough she said "Tach!" Nothing more. And however unplayable her lie, she would hammer away with her niblick until that ball was out of trouble, and half Perthshire with it. If it took her fifteen strokes, no matter; she would tot them up grimly when the putts were down, remark, "This and better may do, this and waur will never do", and stride off to the next tee, gripping her driver like a battle-axe.

As an opponent she was terrifying, not only because she played well, but because she made you aware that this was a personal duel in which she intended to grind you into the turf without pity; if she was six up at the seventeenth she would still attack that last hole as if life depended on it. At first I hated playing with her, but gradually I learned to meet her with something of her own spirit, and if I could never achieve the killer instinct which she possessed, at least I discovered satisfaction in winning, and did so without embarrassment.

As a partner she was beyond price. Strangely enough, when we played as a team, we developed a comradeship closer than I ever felt for any other player; we once even held our own with my father and uncle, who together could have given a little trouble to any golfers anywhere. Even conceding a stroke a hole they were immeasurably better than an aged woman and an erratic small boy, but she was their mother and let them know it; the very way she swung her brassie was a wordless reminder of the second commandment, and by their indulgence, her iron will, and enormous luck, we came all square to the eighteenth tee.

Counting our stroke, we were both reasonably close to the green in two, and my granny, crouching like a bombazine vulture with her mashie-niblick, put our ball about ten feet from the pin. My father, after thinking and clicking his tongue, took his number three and from a nasty lie played a beautiful rolling run-up to within a foot of the hole—a real old Fife professional's shot.

I looked at the putt and trembled. "Dand," said my grandmother. "Never up, never in."

So I gulped, prayed, and went straight for the back of the cup. I hit it, too, the ball jumped, teetered, and went in. My father and uncle applauded, granny said "Aye", and my uncle stooped to his ball, remarking, "Halved hole and match, eh?"

"No such thing," said granny, looking like the Three Fates. "Take your putt."

Nowadays, of course, putts within six inches or so are frequently conceded, as being unmissable. Not with my grandmother; she would have stood over Arnold Palmer if he had been on the lip of the hole. So my uncle sighed, smiled, took his putter, played—and missed. His putter went into the nearest bunker, my father walked to the edge of the green, humming to himself, and my grandmother sniffed and told me curtly to pick up my bag and mind where I was putting my feet on the green.

As we walked back to the clubhouse, she grimly silent as usual, myself exulting, while the post-mortem of father and uncle floated out of the dusk behind us, she made one of her rare observations.

"A game," she said, "is not lost till it's won. Especially with your Uncle Hugh. He is—" and here her face assumed the stern resignation of a materfamilias who has learned that one of the family has fled to Australia pursued by creditors, "—a *trifling* man. Are your feet wet? Aye, well, they won't stay dry long if you drag them through the grass like that."

And never a word did she say about my brilliant putt, but back in the clubhouse she had the professional show her all the three irons he had, chose one, beat him down from seventeen and six to eleven shillings, handed it to me, and told my father to pay for it. "The boy needs a three iron," she said. And to me: "Mind you take care of it." I have taken care of it.

But all this was long ago, and has nothing much to do

with the story of Private McAuslan, that well-known military disaster, golfing personality and caddy extraordinary. Except for the fact that I suppose something of that great old lady's personality stayed with me, and exerted its influence whenever I took a golf club in hand. Not that this was often; as I grew through adolescence I developed a passion for cricket, a love-hate relationship with Rugby, and some devotion to soccer, so that golf faded into the background. Anyway, for all my early training, I wasn't much good, a scratching, turf-cutting 24-handicapper whose drives either went two hundred yards dead straight or whined off at right angles into the wilderness. I was full of what you might call golfing lore and know-how, but in practice I was an erratic slasher, a blasphemer in bunkers, and prone to give up round about the twelfth hole and go looking for beer in the clubhouse.

In the army there was less time than ever for golf, but it chanced that when our Highland battalion was posted back to Scotland from North Africa shortly after the war we were stationed on the very edge of one of those murderous east coast courses where the greens are small and fast, the wind is a howling menace, and the rough is such that you either play straight or you don't play at all. This, of course, is where golf was born, where the early giants made it an art before the Americans turned it into a science, and whence John Paterson strode forth in his blacksmith's apron to partner the future King James II in the first international against England. (That was a right crafty piece of gamesmanship on James's part, too, but it won the match, so there you are.)

In any event, the local committee made us free of their links, and the battalion had something of a golfing revival. This was encouraged by our new Colonel, a

stiffish, Sandhurst sort of man who had decided views
on what was sport and what was not. Our old Colonel
had been a law unto himself: boxing, snooker, billiards-
fives, and working himself into hysterics at battalion
football matches had been his mark, but the new man
saw sport through the pages of *Country Life*. Well, I
mean, he rode horses, shot grouse, and belonged to some
ritzy yacht club on the Forth where they drank pink gin
and wore handkerchiefs in their sleeves. To a battalion
whose notions of games began and ended with a football, this was something rich and strange. But since he
approved of golf, and liked to see his officers taking
advantage of the local club's hospitality, those of us who
could play did so, and a fairly bad showing we made.
Subalterns like myself plowtered our way round and
rejoiced when we broke 90; two of our older majors set
a record in lost balls for a single round (23, including
five found and lost again); the Regimental Sergeant-
Major played a very correct, military game in which the
ball seldom left the fairway but never travelled very far
either; and the M.O. and Padre set off with one set of
clubs and the former's hip flask—their round ended with
the Padre searching for wild flowers and the M.O. lying
in the bracken at the long fourteenth singing "Kishmul's
Galley". It was golf of a kind, if you like, and only the
Adjutant took it at all seriously.

This was probably because he possessed a pair of pre-
war plus fours and a full set of clubs, which enabled
him to put on tremendous side. Bunkered, which he
usually was, he would affect immense concern over
whether he should use a seven or eight iron—would the
wind carry his chip far enough? should he apply top
spin?

"What do you think, Pirie?" he would ask his partner,
who was the officers' mess barman but in private life

had been assistant pro. at a course in Nairn and was the only real golfer in the battalion. "Should I take the seven or the eight?"

"For a' the guid ye are wi' either o' them ye micht as weel tak' a bluidy bulldozer," Pirie would say. Upon which he would be sternly reprimanded for insubordination, the Adjutant would seize his blaster, and after a dozen unsuccessful slashes would snatch up the ball in rage and hurl it frenziedly into the whins.

"It's a' one," Pirie would observe. "Ye'd have three-putted anyway."

"I can't understand it," I once heard the Adjutant say in the mess bar, in that plaintive, self-examining tone which is the hallmark of the truly bum golfer. "I've tried the overlap grip, I've tried the forefinger down the shaft; I've stood up from the ball and I've crouched over it; I've used several stances, with my feet together, my feet apart, and my knees bent—everything! But the putts simply won't go down. Pirie here will confirm me. I don't understand it at all. What do you think, Pirie?"

"Ye cannae bluidy well putt," said the unfeeling Pirie. "That's a' there is to it."

Mess barmen, it need hardly be added, are privileged people, and anyway the Adjutant and Pirie had once stood back to back in an ambush on the Chocolate Staircase, and had an understanding of their own. It was something which the new Colonel would not have fully appreciated, for he had not served with the regiment since before the war, and was as big a stickler for military discipline as long service on the staff could make him. He did not understand the changes which six years of war had wrought, most especially in a Highland regiment, which is a curious organisation in the first place.

It looks terribly military, and indeed it is, but under

the surface a Highland unit has curious currents which are extremely irregular. There is a sort of unspoken yet recognised democracy which may have its roots in clanship, or in the Scottish mercenary tradition, and which can play the devil with rank and authority unless it is properly understood. The new Colonel obviously was unaware of this, or he would not have suddenly ordained, one fine bright morning, that whenever an officer played golf he should have a soldier to caddy for him.

In feudal theory, even in military theory, this was all very well. In the egalitarian atmosphere of a Highland battalion, circa 1947, it was simply not on; our old Colonel wouldn't even have thought of it. Quite apart from the fact that every man in the unit, in that Socialist age, knew his rights and was well aware that caddying wasn't covered by the Army Act—well, you can try getting a veteran of Alamein and Anzio to carry golf clubs for a pink-cheeked one-pipper, but when that veteran has not only learned his political science at Govan Cross but is also a member of an independent and prideful race, you may encounter difficulties. However, the Colonel's edict had gone forth, and after it had been greeted in the mess with well-bred whistles and exclamations of "I *say!*" and "Name o' the wee man!", I was left, as battalion sports officer, to arrange the impressment of suitable caddies.

"The man's mad," I told the Adjutant. "There'll be a mutiny."

"Oh, I don't know," he said. "You could try picking on the simple-minded ones."

"The only simple-minded ones in this outfit are in our own mess," I said. "Can you imagine Wee Wullie's reaction, for example, if he's told to caddy for some of our young hopefuls? He'll run amuck." Wee Wullie was a giant of uncontrolled passions and immense brawn whose answer to any vexing problem was usually a swung fist. "And the rest of them are liable to write to their M.P.s. You don't know the half of it in Headquarter Company; out where the rest of us live it's like a Jacobin literary society."

"Use tact," advised the Adjutant, "and if that fails, try blackmail. But whatever you do, for God's sake don't provoke a disciplinary crisis."

In other words, perform the impossible, and the only normal way to do that was to enlist the Regimental Sergeant-Major, the splendid Mr Mackintosh. But I hesitated to do this; like a scientist on the brink of some shattering experiment, I was fearful of releasing powers beyond my control. So after deep thought I decided to confine my activities to my own platoon, whom I knew, and made a subtle approach to the saturnine Private Fletcher, who was the nearest thing to a shop steward then in uniform. We were soon chatting away on that agreeable officer-man basis which is founded on mutual respect and makes the British Army what it is.

"Fletcher," I said casually, "there are a limited number of openings for Jocks to caddy for the officers when they play golf. It's light work, in congenial surroundings, and those who are fortunate enough to be selected will receive certain privileges, etc., etc. Now those loafers up in Support Company would give their right arms for the chance, but what I say is, what's the use of my being sports officer if I can't swing a few good things for my own chaps, so—"

"Aye, sir," said Fletcher. "Whit's the pey?"

"The pay?"

"Uh-huh. The pey. Whit's the rate for the job?"

This took me aback. It hadn't occurred to me to suggest paying Jocks to caddy, and I was willing to bet it

hadn't occurred to the Colonel either. Fall in the loyal
privates, touching their forelocks by numbers, would be
his idea. But I now saw a way through this embarrassing
problem; after all, I did have a sports fund at my dis-
posal, and a quarter-master who could cook a book to a
turn.

"Well, now," I said, "we ought to be able to fix that
easily enough. Suppose we say about a shilling an
hour . . ." The fund ought to be able to stand that, under
"miscellaneous".

"Aw, jeez, come aff it, sir," said Fletcher respectfully.
"*Two* bob an hour, an' overtime in the evenin's. Double
time Setterdays an' Sundays, an' a hardship bonus for
whoever has tae carry the Adjutant's bag. Yon's a bluidy
disgrace, no kiddin'; the man's no fit tae play on the
street. Ye'll no' get anyone in his right mind tae caddy
for him; it'll have tae be yin o' the yahoos." He fumbled
in his pocket. "I've got a wee list here, sir, o' fellas that
would do, wi' the rates I was mentionin' just now. Wan
or two o' them have played golf theirsel's, so they mebbe
ought tae get two an' six an hour—it'll be kinda professional advice, ye see. But we'll no' press it."

I looked dumbly at him for a moment. "You knew
about this? But, dammit, the Adjutant only mentioned
it half an hour ago . . ."

He looked at me pityingly as I took his list. Of course,
I ought to have known better. All this stuff about Highlanders' second sight is nonsense; it's just first-class
espionage, that's all.

"Well," I said, studying the list, "I don't know about
this. I'm sure it's all very irregular . . ."

"So's the employment o' military personnel ootwith
military duties," said Fletcher smugly. "Think if somebody frae the *Daily Worker* wis tae get word that wee
shilpit Toamy frae the Q.M. store—him wi' the bad feet

—wis humphin' the Adjutant's golf-sticks a' ower the place. They might even get a picture of him greetin'——"

"Quite, quite," I said. "Point taken. All right, two bob an hour, but I want respectable men, understand?"

"Right, sir." Fletcher hesitated. "Would there be a wee allowance, mebbe, for wear an' tear on the fellas' civvy clothes? They cannae dae the job in uniform, and it's no fair tae expect a fella tae spile his glamour pants and long jaicket sclimmin' intae bunkers—"

"They can draw white football shirts and long khaki drills from the sports store," I said. "Now go away, you crimson thief, and see that nobody who isn't on this list ever hears that there's payment involved, otherwise we'll have a queue forming up. I want this thing to work nice and smoothly."

And of course it did. Fletcher had picked eight men, including himself, of sober habit and decent appearance, and the sight of them in their white shirts and khaki slacks, toting their burdens round the links, did the Colonel's heart good to see. It all looked very military and right, and he wasn't to know that they were being subsidised out of battalion funds. In fact, I had quietly informed the Adjutant that if those officers who played golf made an unofficial contribution to the sports kitty, it would be welcome, and the result was that we actually showed a profit.

The Jocks who caddied were all for it. They made money, they missed occasional parades, and they enjoyed such privileges as watching the Adjutant have hysterics while standing thigh-deep in a stream, or hearing the Padre addressing heaven from the midst of a bramble patch. It was all good clean fun, and would no doubt have stayed that way if the new Colonel, zealous for his battalion's prestige, hadn't got ambitious.

He didn't play golf himself, but he took pride in his unit's activities, and it chanced that on one of his strolls across the course he saw Pirie the barman playing against the better of our elderly majors. The major must have been at his best, and Pirie's game was immaculate as usual, so the Colonel, following them over the last three holes, got a totally false impression of the standard of golf under his command. This, he decided, was pretty classy stuff, and it seems that he mentioned this to his friend who commanded the Royals, who inhabited that part of the country. Colonels are forever boasting to each other in this reckless way, whereby their underlings often suffer most exquisitely.

Anyway, the Colonel of the Royals said he had some pretty fair golfers in his mess, and how about a game? Our Colonel, in his ignorance, accepted the challenge. I privately believe that he had some wild notion that because we had caddies in nice white shirts we would have a built-in advantage, but in any event he placed a bet with the Royals' C.O. and then came home to tell the Adjutant the glad news. We were to field ten players in a foursomes match against the Royals, and we were to win.

Now, you may think an inter-regimental golf match is fairly trivial stuff, but when a new and autocratic Colonel is involved, puffed up with regimental conceit, and when the opposition is the Royals, it is a most serious matter. For one thing, the Royals are unbearable. They are tremendously old, and stuffed with tradition and social graces, and adopt a patronising attitude to the rest of the army in general, and other Scottish units in particular. Furthermore, they can play golf—or they could then—and of this the Adjutant was painfully aware.

However, like the good soldier he was, he set about

marshalling his forces, which consisted of making sure
that he personally partnered Pirie.

"We know each other's game, you see," he told me.
"We blend, as it were."

"You mean he'll carry you round on his back," I said.
"You don't fool me, brother. You see that partnering
Pirie is the one chance you've got of being in a winning
pair."

"Look," he said. "I've got to work with the Colonel;
I see him every day, don't I? I've got to salvage some-
thing from what is sure to be a pretty beastly wreck.
Now, how about the second pair? The Padre and the
M.O., eh? They always play together."

"They'll be good for a laugh, anyway," I said. "Unless
the Royals go easy on them out of respect for the clerical
cloth, or the M.O. can get his opponents drunk, they
don't stand a prayer."

"Then there's young Macmillan—he's not bad," said
the Adjutant hopefully. "I saw him hole a putt the other
day. You could partner him yourself."

"Not a chance," I said. "The best he's ever gone round
in is 128, with a following wind. Furthermore he giggles.
I want to succumb with dignity; either I partner the
R.S.M. or you can get yourself another boy."

"Old man Mackintosh, eh?" said the Adjutant. "Well,
he's a steady player, isn't he? Can't think I've ever seen
him in the rough."

"That's why I want him," I said. "I want to play a
few of my shots from a decent lie."

"You've got a rotten, defeatist attitude," said the
Adjutant severely.

"I'm a rotten, defeatist golfer," I said. "So are you,
and so are the rest of us, bar Pirie."

"Ah, yes, Pirie," said the Adjutant, smirking. "He and
I should do not too badly, I think. If I can remember

not to overswing; and I think I'll get the pro. to shave my driver just a teeny fraction—for balance, you know —and get in a bit of practice with my eight iron . . ."

"Come back to earth, Sarazen," I said. "You've still got two couples to find."

We finally settled on our two elderly majors, Second-Lieutenant Macmillan, and Regimental Quartermaster Bogle, a stout and imposing warrant officer who had been known to play a few rounds with the pipe-sergeant. No one knew how they scored, but Bogle used to say off-handedly that his game had rusted a wee bitty since he won the Eastern District Boys' Title many years ago —heaven help us, it must have been when Old Tom Morris was in small clothes—and the pipey would nod sagely and say:

"Aye, aye, Quarters, a wee thing over par the day, just a wee thing, aye. But no' bad, no' bad at all."

Personally I thought this was lying propaganda, but I couldn't prove it.

"It is," admitted the Adjutant, "a pretty lousy team. Oh, well, at least our caddies will look good."

But there he was dead wrong. He was not to know it, but lurking in the background was the ever-present menace of Private McAuslan, now preparing to take a hand in the fate of the battalion golf team.

He was far from my mind on the afternoon of the great match, as the R.S.M. and I stood waiting outside the clubhouse to tee off. Presently my own batman, the tow-headed McClusky, who was caddying for me, arrived on the scene, and shambling behind him was the Parliamentary Road's own contribution to the pollution problem, McAuslan himself.

"What's he doing here?" I demanded, shaken.

"He's come tae caddy," explained McClusky. "See,

there's only eight caddies on the list, an' ten o' ye playin', so Fletcher picked anither two. Him an' Daft Bob Broon."

"Why him?" I hissed, aware that our visitors from the Royals were casting interested glances towards Mc-Auslan, whose grey-white shirt was open to the waist, revealing what was either his skin or an old vest, you couldn't tell which. His hair was tangled and his mouth hung open; altogether he looked as though he'd just completed a bell-ringing stint at Notre Dame.

"Fletcher said it would be a'right."

"I'll talk to Master Fletcher in due course," I said. "But you ought to have known better, at least. Well, you can darn your own socks after this, my lad." I turned to McAuslan. "You," I hissed, "button your shirt and try to look half-decent."

"Ah cannae, sir, but." He pawed unhappily at his insanitary frontage. "The buttons his came aff."

I'd been a fool to mention it, of course. I wondered momentarily if there was time to dismiss him and get a replacement, but the first foursome was already on the tee. "Well, tuck the damned thing in at least, and get hold of yourself. You're caddying for the Regimental Sergeant-Major."

I don't know which of them was hit hardest by this news; probably no two men in the battalion were as eager to shun each other's company. McAuslan went in fear and horror of the majestic Mackintosh; the R.S.M., on the other hand, who had been brought up in the Guards, regarded McAuslan as a living insult to the profession of arms, and preferred to ignore his existence. Now they were in enforced partnership, so to speak. I left them to renew old acquaintance, and went to watch the first shots being exchanged on the tee.

Pirie and the Adjutant were our openers, and when

Pirie hit his drive out of sight you could see the Adjutant smirking approval in a way which invited the onlookers to believe that he, too, was cast in the same grand mould. Poor sap, he didn't seem to realise that he would shortly be scooping great lumps out of the fairway while Pirie gritted his teeth and their opponents looked embarrassed. Not that the Royals looked as though pity was their long suit; it is part of their regimental tradition to look as much like army officers as possible—the type who are to be seen in advertisements for lime juice, or whisky, or some splendid out-of-doors tobacco. They were brown, leathery, moustached upper-crust Anglo-Scots, whose well-worn wind-cheaters and waterproof trousers could have come only from Forsyth's or Rowan's; their wooden clubs had little covers on their heads, their brogues had fine metal spikes, and they called each other Murdoch and Doug. Nowadays they broke stocks or manage export concerns, and no doubt they still play golf extremely well.

Our second pair were Damon and Pythias, the two elderly majors, who took the tee with arthritic moans. Rivals for the same girl when they had been stationed at Kasr-el-Nil before the war, they disliked each other to the point of inseparability, and lived in a state of feud. If they could manage to totter round the eighteen holes they would at least put up a show, which was more than I expected from our third couple, the Padre and the M.O.

They were a sight to see. The M.O., eating pills and wearing gym shoes, was accompanied by a caddy festooned with impedimenta—an umbrella, binoculars, flask, sandwich case and the like. Golf, to the M.O., was not to be taken lightly. The Padre, apart from his denim trousers, was resplendent in a jersey embroidered for him by the market mammies of some St Andrew's Kirk

in West Africa, a souvenir of his missionary days. A
dazzling yellow, it had his name in scarlet on the front
—"Rev. McLeod", it said—while on the back, in many
colours, was the Church of Scotland emblem of the
burning bush, with "Nec tamen consumebatur" underneath. The Padre wouldn't have parted with it for
worlds; he had worn it under his battledress on D-Day,
and intended to be buried in it.

The M.O., breathing heavily, drove off, which consisted of swinging like a Senlac axe-man, overbalancing,
and putting up a ball which, had he been playing
cricket, would have been easily caught at square leg.

"'Gregory, remember thy swashing blow'," quoted
the Padre. "Man, but there's power there, if it could be
harnessed. Don't you worry, Lachlan, I'll see to it", and
he wandered off towards the ball to play the second
shot after his opponents had driven off—which they did,
very long and very straight.

Second-Lieutenant Macmillan and R.Q.M.S. Bogle
were next, Macmillan scraping his drive just over the
brow of the hill fifty yards in front of the tee. Then the
MacNeill–Mackintosh combo took the stage, and as we
walked on to the tee with the Colonels and attendant
minions watching from the clubhouse verandah, I could
hear the R.S.M.'s muttered instructions to the shuffling
McAuslan: ". . . those are the wooden clubs with the
wooden heads; the irons have metal heads. All are
numbered accordin' to their purpose. When I require a
parteecular club I shall call oot the number, and you
will hand it to me, smertly and with care. Is that clear?"

God help you, you optimistic sergeant-major, I
thought, and invited him to tee off—whoever fell flat on
his face in front of the assembled gallery, it wasn't going
to be me. He put a respectable drive over the hill, our
opponents drove immaculately, and we were off, four

golfers, three caddies, and McAuslan shambling behind, watching the R.S.M. fearfully, like a captured slave behind a chariot.

Looking back, I can't say I enjoyed that match. For one thing, I was all too conscious of what was happening in the foursomes ahead of us, and over the first nine at least it wasn't good. From time to time they would come into view, little disheartening tableaux: the M.O. kneeling under a bush, swearing and wrestling with the cap of his flask; R.Q.M.S. Bogle trying to hit a ball which was concealed by his enormous belly, while Macmillan giggled nervously; our elderly majors beating the thick rough with their clubs and reviling each other; the Adjutant's plaintive bleat drifting over the dunes: "I'm awfully sorry, Pirie, I can't imagine what's happened to my mid-irons today; either it's the balance of the clubs or I'm over-swinging. What do you think, Pirie, am I over-swinging?" And so on, while the wind blew gently over the sunlit course, ruffling the bent grass, and the distant sea glittered from its little choppy wavelets; it was a brisk, beautiful backdrop totally out of keeping with the condition of the tortured souls trudging over the links, recharging all their worst emotions and basest instincts in the pursuit of little white balls. It makes you think about civilisation, it really does.

I refer to the emotions of our own side, of course. The Royals, for all I know, were enjoying it. My own personal opponents seemed to be, at any rate. They were of the type I have already described, trim, confident men called Hamilton and Dalgliesh—or it may have been Melville and Runcieman, I can't be sure. They played a confident, rather showy game, with big, erratic drives and carefully-considered chips and putts —which, oddly enough, didn't give them much edge on us. Mackintosh was a steady, useful player, and I'd been worse; we weren't discontented to reach the turn one down.

I had arranged for the pipe-sergeant to station himself at the ninth green, to give progress reports on the other games, and he was bursting with news.

"Sir, sir, the Adjutant and Pirie iss in the lead! They're wan hole up, sir, an' Pirie playin' like God's anointed. The Adjutant iss a shambles, poor soul, and him such a charmin' dancer, but Pirie is carryin' the day. His drives iss like thunderbolts, and his putts is droppin' from wherever. Oh, the elegance of it, and the poor Adjutant broke his driver at the eighth an' him near greetin'. But they're wan up, sir."

"How about the others?"

"The majors is square, but failin' rapidly. I doot Major Fleming'll be to carry home; the endurance is not in him. Bogle an' the boy—Mr Macmillan, that is—are two doon, an' lucky at that, for Bogle's guts is a fearful handicap. They hinder his swing, ye see, and he's vexed. But he's game, for a' that, an' wan o' the Royals he's playin' against has ricked his back, so there's hope yet."

Ahead in one game, square in one, behind in two; it could have been worse. "How about the Padre and the M.O.?"

The pipe-sergeant coughed delicately. "Seven doon, sir, and how they contrived to save two holes, God alone knows. It's deplorable, sir; the M.O. has been nippin' ahint a bush after every hole for a sook at his flask, and iss as gassed as a Ne'erday tinker. The poor Padre has gone awa' into one o' they wee broon things—"

"Into what?"

"Into a dwalm, sir, a revaree, like a trance, ye ken. He wanders, and keeks intae bunkers, and whistles in the Gaelic. There's nae sense in either o' them, sir;

they're lost to ye." He said it much as a Marshal of France might have reported the defeat of an army to Napoleon, sad but stern. "And yerself, sir? One doon? What iss that to such men as yerself and the Major, see the splendid bearin' of him! Cheer up, sir, a MacNeill never cried barley; ye had your own boat in the Flood."

"That was the MacLeans, pipey," I said sadly. The Colonel, I was thinking, wasn't going to like this; by the same process of logic, he wasn't going to like his sports officer. Well, if Pirie kept his winning streak, and the two old majors lasted the distance—it was just possible that the R.S.M. and I might achieve something, who knew? But the outlook wasn't good, and I drove off at the tenth in no high spirits.

And it was at this point that Private McAuslan began to impose his personality on the game. Knowing about McAuslan, you might think that an odd way of putting it—interfere with something, yes; wreck, frustrate or besmirch—all these things he could do. But even with his talent for disaster, he had never been what you could call a controlling influence—until the R.S.M., playing our second shot at the tenth, for once hooked, and landed us deep in tiger country.

We thrashed about in the jungle, searching, but there wasn't a hope, and with the local five-minute rule in operation we had to forfeit the hole. Personally, if it had been our opponents, I'd have suggested they drop a new ball and forfeit a stroke, but there it was. We were two down, and the R.S.M. for once looked troubled.

"I'm extremely sorry aboot that, sir," he confided to me. "Slack play. No excuse. I'm extremely sorry."

I hastened to reassure him, for I guessed that perhaps to the R.S.M. this match was even more important than to the rest of us. When your life is a well-ordered, immaculate success, as his was, any failure begins to look

important. Perfection was his norm; being two down
was not perfection, and losing a ball was inexcusable.

Meanwhile, I was aware of voices behind us, and one
of them was McAuslan's. He had been quiet on the
outward half, between terror of the R.S.M. and his own
inability to distinguish one club from another—for he
was illiterate, a rare but not unknown thing in the Army
of those days. Perhaps his awe of Mackintosh had
diminished slightly—the serf who sees his overlord
grunting in a bunker gets a new slant on their relationship, I suppose. Anyway, the fearful novelty of his
situation having worn off, he was beginning to take an
interest, and McAuslan taking an interest was wont to
be garrulous.

"Hey, Chick," I heard him say, addressing my caddy.
"Whit we no' finishing this hole fur?"

"We've loast it," said McClusky. "We loast wir ba'."

"So whit? Hiv we no' got anither yin?"

"Aye, we've got anither yin, but if ye lose a ba' ye
lose the hole. It's the rules."

A pause. Then: "Ah, —— the rules. It's no' fair. Sure
it's no fair, huh, Chick?"

"Aw, Goad," said McClusky, "Ah'm tellin' ye, it's the
rule, ye dope. Same's at fitba'."

"Weel, Ah think it's daft," said McAuslan. "Look, at
fitba', if a man kicks the ba' oot the park—"

"All right, McAuslan, pipe down," I said. I knew that
one of the few abstract ideas ever to settle in that
neanderthal mind was a respect for justice—his sense
of what was "no' fair" had once landed him in a court
martial—but this was no time for an address by Mc-
Auslan, Q.C. "Just keep quiet, and watch the ball. If
you'd done it last time we might not have lost the hole."
Which wasn't strictly fair, but I was punished for it.

"Quaiet, please," said one of our opponents. "No tock-

ing on the tee, if you don't mind." And he added.
"Thenk-you."

The crust of it was, he hadn't even teed up. Suddenly
I realised what had been wrong with this game so far—
I'd had half my mind on the other matches, half on my
own play: I hadn't really noticed our opponents. And
that's no good. Ask Dr Grace or Casey Stengel or my
Highland granny—you've *got* to notice the opposition,
and abominate them. That totally unnecessary "Quaiet,
please" had made it easy.

Our opponents drove off, respectably, and Mackintosh,
subconsciously trying to redeem his lost ball, tried a
big one, instead of his usual cautious tee-shot. It soared
away splendidly, but with slice written all over it; it
was going to land well among the whins.

"Keep your eye on it!" I shouted, and McAuslan, full
of zeal, bauchled masterfully across the tee, dragging his
bag, his eyes staring fixedly into the blue, roaring:

"Ah see it! Ah've spotted the b——! Don't worry, sir!
Ah see—"

Unfortunately it was one of those high plateau tees,
with a steep drop to whins and rough grass at the start
of the fairway. McAuslan, blind to everything except
the soaring ball, marched into the void and descended
with a hideous clatter of clubs and body, to which
presently he added flowers of invective picked up on
the Ibrox terracing. He crawled out of the bushes,
blaspheming bitterly, until he realised the R.S.M.'s
cold eye was on him; then he rose and limped after the
ball.

The opponent who had rebuked me—I think of him
as Melville—chuckled.

"Thet's a remarkable individual," he said to me.
"Wherever did you get him?" A fair enough question,
from anyone meeting McAuslan for the first time, but

with just a hint of patronage, perhaps. "You ott to keep an aye on him, before he hurts himself," went on Melville jocularly. "Aye don't think he's doing anything for your pårtner's peace of mind, eether."

It might have been just loud enough for Mackintosh to hear; I may have been wrong, but I think I know gamesmanship when I hear it. Coming on top of the "Quaiet, please", it just settled my hate nicely; from that moment the tension was on, and I squared up to that second shot in the deep rough, determined to hit the green if it killed me. Four shots later we were in a bunker, conceding a hole that was hopelessly lost. Three down and seven to play.

Not a nice position, and McAuslan didn't help things. Perhaps his fall had rattled him, or more probably his brief sally into the limelight had made him more than normally self-conscious. He accidentally trod in the tee-box at the twelfth, and had to have his foot freed by force (the fact that Melville muttered something about "accident-prone" did nothing for my temper). Then he upended the R.S.M.'s bag, and we had to wait while he retrieved the clubs, scrabbling like a great beast with his shirt coming out. I forced myself to be calm, and managed a fairish drive to the edge of the short twelfth green; Mackintosh chipped on well, and we halved in three.

The thirteenth was one of those weird holes by which games of golf are won and lost. Our position was fairly hopeless—three down and six—and possibly because of that we played it like champions. The R.S.M. drove straight, and for once he was long; I took my old whippy brassie with its wooden shaft, drove from my mind the nameless fear that McAuslan would have an apoplectic fit or shoot me in the back while I was in the act of swinging, and by great good luck hit one of those perfect shots away downhill. It flew, it bounced, it ran, trickling between the bunkers to lie nicely just a yard on to the green.

Melville and Co. were in dire straits. They took three and were still short of the green, and I was counting the hole won when Melville took out his number seven iron and hit the bonniest chip I ever hope to see; of course it was lucky, landing a yard short of the flag with lots of back spin, and then running straight as a die into the cup, but that's golf. They were down in four, we were on in two, and Mackintosh had a fifteen-yard putt.

He strode ponderously on to the green, looked at the ball as though to ask its name, rank and number, and held out his hand for his putter. McAuslan rummaged fearfully, and then announced tremulously:

"It's no' here, sir."

And it wasn't. Sulphurous question and whimpering answer finally narrowed the thing down to the point where we realised it must have fallen out when Mc-Auslan, Daedalus-like, had tried to defy gravity at the eleventh tee. He was driven, with oaths and threats, to fetch it, and we waited in the sunlight, Melville and his friend saying nothing pointedly, until presently Mc-Auslan hove in view again, looking like the last survivor of Fort Zinderneuf staggering home, dying of thirst. But he had the club.

"Ah'm awfu' sorry, sir. It must hiv fell oot." He wiped his sweating grey nose audibly, and the R.S.M. took the putter without a word, addressed the ball briefly, and sent it across the huge waste of green dead true, un-deviating, running like a pup to its dinner, plopping with a beautiful mellow sound into the tin.

(It's a strange thing, but when I think back to that heroic, colossal putt—or to any other moment in that game, for that matter—I see in my imagination the

R.S.M., not clothed in the mufti which I know he must
have been wearing, but resplendent in full regimentals,
white spats, kilt, dress tunic and broadsword, with a
feather bonnet on top. I *know* he wasn't wearing them,
but he should have been.)

And as we cried our admiration, I thought to myself,
we're only two down now. And five holes to go. And I
heard again that old golfing maxim: "Two up and five
never won a match." Well, it might come true, given
luck.

It certainly began to look like it, for while our drives
and approaches were level at the fourteenth, the R.S.M.
played one of his canny chips while our opponents
barely found the green. Their putt was feebly short, and
mine teetered round the hole, took a long look in, and
finally went down. One up and four.

The fifteenth was a nightmare hole, a par-three where
you played straight out to sea, hoping to find a tiny
green perched above the beach, with only a ribbon of
fairway through the jungle. This was where Mackintosh's cautious driving was beyond price; I trundled on
a lamentable run-up that missed the guarding bunker
by a whisker, and then Melville, panicking, put his
approach over the green and, presumably, into the
North Sea. All square with three to play.

For the first time I was enjoying myself; I felt we had
them on the run, whereupon my Presbyterian soul
revolted and slapped me on the wrists, urging me to be
calm. So I drove cautiously and straight, the R.S.M.
put us within pitching distance, and my chip just stayed
on the back of the green. Melville played the like into a
bunker, they took three to get pin-high, and the R.S.M.'s
putt left me nothing to do but hole a twelve-incher. For
the first time we were in front. And only two holes
remained.

The seventeenth was the first half of a terribly long haul to the clubhouse. It and the eighteenth were par fives, where our opponents' longer hitting ought to tell. But Melville's partner duffed his drive, and while we broke no records in getting to the edge of the green in five, he and his partner undertook a shocking safari into the rough on both sides, and were still off the green in six. I was trembling slightly as I chipped on, and more by luck than judgement I left it within a foot of the cup. Unless they sank their approach, which was unthinkable, we had the match won. I glanced at the R.S.M. His face was wooden, as usual, but as we waited for their shot his fingers were drumming on the shaft of his putter.

Melville's partner, hand it to him, was ready to die game. 'This goes in," he said, shaping up to his ball, which was on the wrong side of a bunker, fifteen yards from the flag. "Pin out, please."

And Private McAuslan, the nearest caddy, ambled across the green to remove the flag.

I should have known, of course; I should have taken thought. But I'd forgotten McAuslan in the excitement of the game; vaguely I had been aware of his presence, when he sniffed, or grunted, or dropped the clubs, or muttered, "Aw, jeez, whit a brammer" when we hit a good shot, or "Ah, ——", when our opponents did. But he hadn't broken his leg, or gone absent, or caught beri-beri, or done anything really McAuslan-like. Now he tramped across to the flag, his paw outstretched, and I felt my premonition of disaster too late.

He claimed afterwards it was a wasp, but as the Adjutant said, it must have been a bot-fly, or maybe a vulture: no sane wasp would have gone near him, in his condition. Whatever it was, he suddenly leaped, swatting and cursing, he stumbled, and his great, flat, ugly, doom-laden foot came down on our ball, squashing it into the turf.

I think I actually screamed. Because the law is the law, and if your caddy touches your ball in play, let alone tries to stamp the damned thing through to Australia, you forfeit the hole. Even Melville, I'll swear, had compassion in his eyes.

"Dem bed luck," he said to me. "Aym offly sorry, but thet puts us all square again."

McAuslan, meanwhile, was gouging our ball out of the green, as a hungry boar might root for truffles. Presently, from the exclamations around, he gathered that somehow he had erred; when he understood that he had cost us the hole, and probably the game, his distress was pitiful to see and disgusting to hear. But what could you say to him? It had all been said before, anyway, to no avail. Poor unwashed blundering soul, it was just the way he was made.

So certain victory had been taken from us, and now all was to play for at the last hole, where the pipe-sergeant was skipping with excitement on the tee. On hearing how we stood he sent a runner post-haste to Aix with the news, and then delivered himself.

Unbelievably, of the other four games we had won two and lost two, and but for the M.O.'s drunken folly we might even have been ahead 3–1. Pirie and the Adjutant had won, two and one ("and oh, the style of yon Pirie, sir! Whaur's yer Wullie Turnesa noo, eh?"). The two elderly majors, against all the odds, had triumphed at the eighteenth by one hole; it appeared that the corpulent Major Fleming, about to give up the struggle at the fifteenth, had been roused by his partner's taunt that the girl in Kasr-el-Nil had said that she couldn't abide fat men, and had told him (the partner) that she could never love a man as overweight as

Fleming, who would certainly be dead of a stroke before he was forty. Inflamed, Fleming had carried all before him, and even with the Padre and M.O. going down to cataclysmic defeat, 9 and 7, the overall prospects had looked not bad. Macmillan and Bogle had fought back to level terms ("and auld Bogle wi' his guts in a sling and pechin' sore, sore") and at the sixteenth one of their opponents, whom the pipey had earlier reported as suffering from muscle strain, had wrenched his shoulder.

He had been about to give up and concede the game, when the Padre, happening by from the scene of his own rout, had suggested that our M.O., who had taken his flask for a sleep in the rough, be summoned to examine the sufferer. They roused the M.O. from beneath a bush, and after focusing unsteadily on the affected part he had announced: "In my professional opinion this man cannot be moved without imperilling his life. Call an ambulance." Alarmed, they had asked him what the Royal was suffering from, and he had replied: "Alcoholic poisoning", and then collapsed himself into a bunker. So indignant had the injured Royal— a senior and extremely stiffish company commander— been that he had insisted on carrying on, and Bogle and Macmillan had lost, two down.

So it was up to the R.S.M. and me to win or lose the whole shooting-match, and as I looked at the huge eighteenth, with its broad fairway just made for the big driving of our opponents, I almost gave up hope. The worst of it was, if it hadn't been for that grubby moron's great flat feet we would have been walking home now, with the thing in the bag; he was mumping dolefully somewhere in the background. I knew I was silly, feeling so upset over a mere game, but what would you? One does.

I watched Melville drive off, and he must have been

feeling the pressure, for he hooked shockingly into a clump of firs. Now's your chance, I thought joyfully, and taking a fine easy swing I topped my drive a good twenty yards down the fairway. Shattered, I watched the R.S.M. prepare to play the second; he had said not a word during the McAuslan débâcle, but for once there was the beginning of a worried frown on the great brow, and with cause, for he sliced his shot away to the high outcrop of rock which ran between the fairway and the sea. The ball pinged among the crags, and then vanished on to the crest, far out in badman's territory. To make it worse, Melville's partner hit a colossal spoon from the trees, leaving them only a longish iron to the green.

This was plainly the end, I thought, as I set off up the bluff in search of the ball, with McClusky trailing behind. We tramped what seemed miles over the springy turf, and found the ball, nicely cocked up on a tuft with the ground falling away sharply ahead to the wide fairway, and three hundred yards off the green, hemmed in by broad deep bunkers. It was a lovely lie, downhill and wide open save for a clump of boulders about two hundred yards off on the right edge of the fairway; there was a following wind, the sea was sparkling, the sun was warm, and everything was an invitation to beat that ball to kingdom come and beyond. Anyway, there was nothing to lose, so I unshipped the old brassie, took a broad stance, waggled the clubhead, did everything wrong, lifted my heel, raised my head, turned my body, and lashed away for dear life. And so help me I leaned upon that ball, and I smote it, so that it rose like a dove in the Scriptures, whining away with an upward trajectory beyond the ken of man, and flew screaming down the wind.

I've never hit one like it, and I never will again. It

was the Big One, the ultimate, and no gallery thundering with applause could have acknowledged it more
appropriately than my own ruptured squawk of astonishment and McClusky's reverent cry of: "Jayzus!" For one
fearful moment I thought it was going to develop a late
slice, but it whanged into the clump of rocks, kicked
magnificently to a huge height as it skidded on, fell
within thirty yards of the green, and rolled gently out of
sight somewhere beside the right-hand bunker.

We hurried down to join the others on the fairway,
where Melville was unlimbering his three iron. He hit a
reasonable shot, but was well short; his partner's seven
was way too high, and plumped into the short rough
just off the green to left. My spirits soared; we were in
business again with a stroke in hand, assuming the
R.S.M. had a reasonable lie, which seemed probable.
We made for the right-hand bunker; I thought I must be
just short of it—and then my heart sank. We were in it;
right in.

Foul trolls from the dark ages had dug that bunker.
It was just off the green, a deep, dark hideous pit fringed
by gorse, with roots straggling under its lips, and little
flat stones among the powdery sand. My great, gorgeous
brassie shot had just reached it, so that the ball was
nestling beside a root, with just room for a man to
swing, and eight feet of bank baring its teeth five yards
in front of him. I've seen bunkers, and bad lies in them,
but this was the nadir.

We looked, appalled, and then that great man the
R.S.M. climbed down into the depths. McAuslan, hover-
ing on the bunker's edge, clubs at the high port, dropped
everything as usual, but the R.S.M. simply snapped:
"Number nine"; even he looked like one on whom the
doom has come. He waited, hand out, eyes fixed on the
barely-visible tip of the flag, while McAuslan rummaged

among the irons on the grass, and handed one down to him. The R.S.M. took the club, and addressed the ball.

It was hopeless, of course; Nicklaus might have got out in one, but I doubt it. The R.S.M. was just going through the motions; he addressed the ball, swung down, and then I saw his club falter in mid-descent, an oath such as I had never heard sprang to his lips, but he was too late to stop. The club descended in a shower of sand, the ball shot across the bunker with frightful speed, hit a root, leaped like a salmon, curved just over the lip of the bunker, bounced, hung, and trickled away down the steep face of the bank on to the green. For a minute I thought it was going in, but it stopped on the very lip of the hole while the sounds of joy and grief from the people wildly rose.

For a moment I could only stare, amazed. I was aware that Melville was chipping on a yard short, and that his partner was holing the putt; they were down in six. I had a tiny putt, two inches at most, for a five and victory, and for the first time in that game the shade of my grandmother asserted herself, reminding me of Uncle Hugh, and chickens unwisely counted. "Never up, never in," I thought, and crouched over the ball; I tapped it firmly in, and that was the ball game.

The Royals were extremely nice about it; splendid losers they were, and there was much good-natured congratulation on the green itself, from our immediate opponents and the other players as well. I detached myself and looked for the R.S.M., but he was not in sight; I went over to the scene of his great shot, and there he was, still standing in the bunker, like a great tweed statue, staring at the club in his hand. And before him, Caliban to Prospero, McAuslan crouched clutching the bag.

"McAuslan," the R.S.M. was saying. "You gave me this club."

"Aye—eh, aye, sir." He was snuffling horribly.

"What club did I require you to give me?"

"Ra number nine, sir."

"And what club did you give me?"

McAuslan, hypnotised, whimpered: "Oh, Goad, Ah dunno, sir."

"This, McAuslan," said the R.S.M. gravely, "is nott a number nine. It is, in fact, a number two. What is called a driving iron. It is not suitable for bunker shots."

"Zat a fact, sir?"

The R.S.M. took a deep breath and let it out again. He was looking distinctly fatigued.

"Return this club to the bag," he said, "put the bag in my quarters, go to the sergeants' mess—the back door—and tell the barman on *my* instructions to supply you with one pint of beer. That's all for now—right, move!"

McAuslan hurled himself away, stricken dumb by fear and disbelief. As he clambered out of the bunker the R.S.M. added:

"Thank you for bein' my caddy, McAuslan."

If McAuslan heard him, I'm sure he didn't believe what he heard.

The R.S.M. climbed out heavily, and gave me his slight smile. "Thank you, sir, for a most enjoyable partnership; a very satisfactory concluding putt, if I may say so."

"Major," I said—my emotion and admiration were such that I had slipped into the old ranker's form of address—"any infant could have holed it. But that bunker shot—man, that was incredible!"

"Incredible indeed, sir. Did you see what I played it wi'? A number two iron—a flat-faced club, sir! Dear me, dear me. By rights I should be in there yet—and I would have been thanking McAuslan for that, I can tell you!"

"Well, thank goodness he did give you the wrong club. You couldn't have played a finer shot, with a nine or anything else."

"Indeed I couldn't. Indeed I couldn't." He shook his head. "By George, Mr MacNeill, we had the luck with us today."

"Hand of providence," I said lightly.

"No, sir," said the R.S.M. firmly. "Let us give credit where it is due. It was the hand of Private McAuslan."

His Majesty
says
good-day

Nowadays, if ever my thoughts stray back across the years to Private McAuslan, I can feel a strange expression stealing across my face. I know, without glancing in the mirror, that I'm beginning to look like a large and truculent Uriah Heep, cringing but defiant, as though uncertain whether to grovel or hit out blindly. It's a conditioned reflex, born from the countless times I've stood at the elbows of outraged colonels and company commanders, making placatory noises and muttering balefully that I'm sure the accused won't do it again, given a second chance. (He did, though, every time.)

This is the penalty you pay for commanding the dumbest and dirtiest soldier in the world: on the one hand you have to chastise and oppress him for the good of his soul, and on the other you have to plead his cause and defend him, almost to the point of defiance, from the wrath of higher authority. The devil's advocating I did for that man would have earned a standing ovation from Lincoln's Inn; I can't count the passionate appeals or the shameless distortions of King's Regulations that I have advanced to excuse his tardiness, stupidity, dirt, negligence, and occasionally drunkenness and absence without leave. Not, admittedly, with great success. I would only add that if any young lawyer wants practice in defending deservedly lost causes, let him assume responsibility for McAuslan for one calendar month. After that, he'll have nothing to learn.

I suppose, recalling the time I sweated through his court martial for disobedience, or the occasion when he fell prone in an intoxicated condition, wearing only his shirt and one army boot, before an officer of general rank, that his last clash with military authority was trivial by comparison. I only remember it because it was the last, and took place, appropriately, on the day before he and I were demobilised. (There was a kind of awful kismet about the fact that he was with me to the end.) Yet, paltry though it was, it was essentially McAuslan, in that it demonstrated yet again his carelessness, negligence, and indiscipline, and at the same time his fine adherence to principle.

I had just taken my final company orders in the office, and was sitting reflecting solemnly that tomorrow I would be a soldier no more, and from that my grasshopper mind started musing on how certain other military men must have felt when their tickets finally came through. Not the great martial names; not the Wellingtons and Napoleons and Turennes, but some of those others who, like me, had been what Shakespeare called warriors for the working day—the conscripts, the volunteers, the civilians who followed the drum and went to war in their time, and afterwards, with luck, picked up their discharges and back money and went home. Not soldiers at all, really, and quite undistinguished militarily—people like Socrates and Ben Jonson, Lincoln and Cobbett, Bunyan and Edgar Allen Poe, Gibbon and Cervantes, Chaucer and John Knox and Daniel Boone and Thomas Cromwell. (McAuslan was trouble enough, but I'd hate to take responsibility for a platoon consisting of that lot.)

And yet, I found it comforting to think that they too, like McAuslan and me—and perhaps you—had once stood nervously on first parade in ill-fitting kit, with their new boots hurting, feeling lost and a long way from home, and had done ablutions fatigue, and queued for the canteen and cookhouse, and worried over the state of their equipment, and stood guard on cold, wet nights, and been upbraided (and doubtless upbraided others in their turn) as idle bodies and dozy men, and thought longingly of their discharge, and generally shared that astonishing experience which, for some reason, men seem to prize so highly. Having been a soldier. It doesn't matter what happens to them afterwards, or how low or high they go, they never forget that ageless company they once belonged to. And if you think that there is not a special link between McAuslan and Socrates and Chaucer and Abe Lincoln, you are dead wrong.

I had just got to the point in my reverie where I was assuring the assembled Athenians that McAuslan's habitual uncleanliness had probably rendered him immune to poison, when I heard the voice of the man himself raised raucously in the company store across the way. Not that that was unusual, but the form of words was novel.

"That's mines," he was protesting. "That's ma private property. Sno' yours. Smines. An' Ah'm bluidy well keepin' it, see? Ah've peyed for it!"

"What d'ye mean, paid for it? When did you ever pay for anything, McAuslan?"

I recognised the voice of young Sergeant Baxter—the same Baxter who, as an over-zealous corporal, had recently been responsible for McAuslan's court martial. That McAuslan had escaped untarnished had merely confirmed the evil relations between them. Privately, I didn't care for Baxter; he was too officious, but he knew his stuff and was keen, and when Sergeant Telfer had returned to civilian life—as a hotel porter, and the hotel was lucky, in my opinion—it would have been unfair to deny Baxter his third tape. But he was woefully short of experience still, as his next words showed.

"And get your heels together when you talk tae me, McAuslan!" His voice was shrill. "An' you address me as 'sergeant'!"

"That'll be right!" roared McAuslan. "Ah can jist see me. Ye're no' comin' the acid wi' me, *Sergeant*—Ah want it back, and I want it noo!"

"Well, ye're no' gettin' it, so fall oot!" snapped Baxter, and I decided to intervene before they fell to brawling.

"What's all the noise, sergeant?" I said, as I went into the store, and Baxter came rapidly to attention. He was pink with outrage, a pleasing contrast to the pastel grey of McAuslan's contorted features. The greatest walking disaster to befall the British Army since Ancient Pistol was modishly clad in a suit of outsize denims in which he appeared to have been scraping the Paris sewers, but his fists were clenched and he was obviously on the brink of unlawful assault of a superior.

"It's this—this man, sir!" said Baxter unnecessarily. "He's trying to lay claim to Army property!"

That was new; McAuslan's normal behaviour with War Department equipment was to lose or defile it as quickly as possible. As it transpired, in this case he had done both.

"It's ma bay'net, sir!" He looked to me in dishevelled appeal. "This bas—, *Sarn't* Baxter—he'll no gie it back tae me. An' it's mines! Ah've peyed for it!"

And sure enough, Baxter was holding a sheathed bayonet, one of the old sword type with the locking-

ring that went on the short Lee Enfield, since super-
seded by other marks, although there were still a number
of them about.

"Haud yer tongue, McAuslan," said Baxter, and to
me: "He's due for demobilisation tomorrow, sir, and I
was seein' that he handed in all his kit properly—it's in
a disgraceful state, sir, there's all kinds o' things missin',
an' nae foresight on his rifle, an' the barrel red rotten wi'
rust, too—"

"Hold on a shake," I said, puzzled. "I didn't know
you were due out tomorrow, McAuslan." I had been
acting company commander for the past three weeks,
and had lost track of my platoon's domestic affairs.
"What's your number?"

"14687347PrivateMcAuslansah!"

"Your demob. number," I said patiently.

"Oh. Hey. Aye. Eh— 57, sir."

It was the same as mine, which was curious. "But
you've been in the Army longer than I have—you were
in the desert in '42. How come you weren't demobbed
long ago?"

He pawed uncertainly with his hooves, ran a hand
through his Gorgon locks—something that I hoped was
a piece of old string fell out—and said uneasily:

"Weel, see, sir, it's like this. When Ah j'ined up, Ah
got back-squadded a few times—ye know? An'—"

"Back-squadded?" scoffed Baxter. "I would think so.
It took them two years tae learn you to slope arms."

"Ah got ma bluidy knees broon, onywye!" McAuslan
rounded on him. "More'n you ever did! Niver saw an
angry German, you—"

"That'll do, McAuslan," I said. "Go on."

He muttered and looked at the floor. "An' Ah did a
bit o' time, too—the glass-hoose at Stirlin'." Memory
stirred his shuffled features into vengeful patterns.

"There was this rotten big sarn't inna Black Watch, right pig he wis, an' he had a down on me, an' he sortit me oot, and got me the jail. Oh, he was a right swine o' a man, so he wis—"

"Yes, I see," I said. "And you're going out tomorrow?" Champagne at the War Office tonight, I thought. "And what's all this about a bayonet?"

"It's mines," he said doggedly, glowering at the weapon in Baxter's hand. "But Ah lost it, a while back, an' they made me pey for it—stopped it oot ma money, they did." He blinked piteously at me, like a widow evicted. "They gie'd me anither bayonet—that's it ower there, wi the rest o' ma kit." He pointed to a mouldering heap lying on the floor on a torn ground-sheet; there was what looked like a large rusty nail among the debris, and I recognised it as one of the new pig-sticker bayonets.

"How the hell did it get in that condition?" I demanded.

"Ah dunno." He wiped his nose audibly. "Ah think it must hae been the damp."

He met my speechless glare, and wilted. "Ah'm sorry, sir, like. Ah'll maybe gie it a wee clean." And he began rooting through his military effects, like a baboon poking among twigs.

"Come out of that!" I exclaimed hastily. "Leave it alone; the less it's—disturbed, the better. Now, what about this other bayonet?" I indicated the weapon in Baxter's hand.

"Well, sir, it's mines, like Ah'm sayin'. See, Ah lost it, two year ago, in the Tripoli barracks, an' had tae pey for it but Ah found it again the ither day, when Ah wis sortin' oot ma kit for tae hand in tae the quartermaster. There it wis, wrapped up in a pair o' ma auld drawers at the bottom o' ma kitbag." He beamed through his grime, while I made the appalling deduction that the lower strata of his kitbag had lain undisturbed for two long years, old drawers and heaven knew what besides. I was just glad I hadn't been there when he finally opened it all up; it must have been like excavating a catacomb.

"But, see, sir," he went on earnestly. "Ah've handed in the pig-sticker they issued me wi' when Ah lost ma auld bayonet. An' Ah peyed for that auld bayonet. So noo that Ah've found it again, it belangs tae me. Sure that's right, sir?"

This sounded like logic. I looked at Baxter.

"He's got a point," I said.

"But, sir!" Baxter protested. "It's still Army issue. He—he cannae *buy* War Department weapons. I'm sure of that. I never heard of such a thing, sir."

Neither had I—but that's my McAuslan. If you've never heard of it—not so fast. He's probably done it.

"Well, since he has paid for it," I said, "at least he's entitled to his money back."

"Ah'm no' wantin' ma money back," proclaimed Mc-Auslan. "Ah want ma bay'net. Ah paid for that bay'net. Smines. Sno' yours—"

"Shut up," said Baxter indignantly. "Ye're no' gettin' it."

"Aw, sure Ah am, sir? He'd niver've known it wis there, even, if he hadnae come pokin' his nose in when Ah wis sortin' oot ma things." You're a better man than I am, Baxter, I thought. "He's got nae right tae try tae tak' it off me. Onywye, two o' the boys that wis in ma platoon in the desert got keepin' their side-arms, when they wis invalided oot in '42. Major MacRobert let them; he wis oor company commander then."

Trust Big Mac. His company hadn't been a company to him; it had been a fighting tail.

"But you can get it credited to you, in money," I said.

"Ah want the bay'net, sir. Ah had it a long time. Ah wis awfy sorry when I lost it." He scratched himself unhappily. "Ah had yon bay'net since Ah j'ined up at Maryhill. Had it in a' sorts o' places. Inna desert, too. Sure an' Ah did."

All sorts of places, I knew, covered Tobruk, Alamein, and Cameron Ridge. I remembered the kukri, carefully oiled and polished, that lay at the bottom of my own trunk.

"I think we could let him keep it," I said after a moment, "and just forget about it, Sergeant Baxter."

"Well, sir," he began doubtfully, but even he wasn't looking quite so adamant. "It's a dangerous weapon, sir—I don't know if it's legal . . . the police . . ."

"We needn't worry about that," I said. What Baxter meant was that to allow cold steel into the hands of a Glasgow man is tantamount to running guns to the Apaches, but I couldn't see McAuslan flourishing his bayonet in gang warfare. He wasn't the type—and uncharitably I reflected that the gangs were probably pretty choosy who they admitted, anyway.

Baxter held it out to him, and McAuslan took it, dropped it, cursed, scrabbled it up, wiped his nose, cleared his throat thunderously, and said, "Ta."

"Carry on, McAuslan," I said, and just to remind him that it wasn't Christmas I added: "And now you've got it, you can clean the dam' thing."

He shambled off—and perhaps it was association of ideas, but when I went back to my billet the first thing I did was to get my broadsword out of the cupboard and look it over. I'd never used it, of course, although it had come close to drawing blood—mine—on one occasion. Back in North Africa, the old Colonel had been inflamed by something he had read in a book about Rob Roy; it

had said, he told us, that in the old days many Highlanders had worn their broadswords on their backs, with
the hilt at the right shoulder, so that they could whip
them out more quickly than from the hip. We would do
this on ceremonial occasions, and the English regiments
would go green with envy. So he had us out behind the
mess, practising, and how the Adjutant didn't decapitate
himself remains a mystery. Even the Colonel had to
admit, reluctantly, that to have all his officers minus
their right ears would present an unbalanced appearance, so the idea was shelved.

Anyway, even if I hadn't drawn it since, there it was
—the claymore, the great sword. You're an odd kind of
Highlander if you can slip your hand inside that beautiful basket-hilt without thinking of Quebec and Waterloo
and Killiecrankie and Culloden and feeling the urge to
kick off your shoes. I'd have to turn it over to the pipe-
sergeant, now that I was leaving.

Naturally, I had mixed feelings about that, too. Perhaps I'd been looking forward for so long to being a
civilian again that now it came as an anti-climax. When
I'd been called up as a conscript during the war it had
been a great adventure; I'd been an eager eighteen,
brought up on war movies and Stout-hearted Stories for
Boys, I'd wanted to get into it, my friends were going
into uniform, the Germans and Japanese patently needed
sorting out, and I genuinely wanted to fight for my
country. Soldiering was also obviously preferable to
swotting in a university (which had turned me down,
anyway).

And I suppose I had known, at the back of my mind,
that when it was all over I would want to look back and
say I'd been in it. (No doubts about survival, you notice.)
As Dr Johnson pointed out, a man who hasn't soldiered
envies the man who has. Illogical, no doubt—immoral,

even, by today's standards—but understandable. My own guess is that old Sam privately regretted not being out in the '45 himself, if only for the free beer and conversation.

But if my initial boyish enthusiasm had never quite rubbed off—although I'll confess there was one night outside Meiktila, with the Japanese White Tigers fooling about round our observation post, when it had worn fairly thin—it had been modified. You could not serve in the British wartime army without being infected by 'ticket' mania—in other words, the anticipation of your eventual discharge. I'd dreamed about it from Derby to Deolali, from freezing parades in Durham to sweltering route-marches in Bengal; on the lower decks of troopers, with the hammock of Grandarse Green slung perilously two inches above me and five hundred bodies snoring close-packed around us; on night stags in Burma when the "up-you" beasts croaked in the jungle and the moon-shadows hypnotised you as they crept towards your rifle-pit; in steamy Northern Naafis, where you hunched miserably over your mug of tea and spam-sandwich with damp serge chafing your neck; in the white-washed stuffiness of my subaltern's billet in Libya, when I lay awake wondering why my platoon seemed to find me an object of derision and dislike—in any of these places, if you had offered me my ticket I'd have snapped your hand off. (But I wouldn't have missed it, not any of it.)

However, dreaming of your ticket is one thing; picking it up is another. Four years is a long time, when it covers the span from boyhood to manhood; you get used to the Army, and provided you'd come through in one piece, and your loved ones likewise, you could look back and say it hadn't been a bad war. That may sound terrible—when I think of those slow-motion moments south of the Irrawady, and the Japanese corpse smell, and our own dead wrapped in blood-stained blankets, it sounds downright obscene—but it's what my generation thought, and perhaps still does. Not, mark you, that we'd want to do it again, and the idea of our children doing it is simply unthinkable.

At any rate, in the last few months before my demobilisation I had pondered on getting out, and at one time had come close to staying in. That had been the old Colonel's fault. Shortly before his own retirement he had loafed into my office one day, ostensibly to inspect some barrack-room repairs, but in fact to do his Ancient Mariner act. He had cornered me, discoursed at length on the joys of a soldier's life, reviewed my own service so far, and hinted that, while permanent commissions were not easy to come by, a word or two in the right place. . . . It was not put anything like as bluntly as that, and took about half an hour, while he sat, puffing at his lovat pipe, dusting tobacco fragments off his kilt, one leg crossed over the other, and wrapping his message up elegantly in reminiscence of service life, from Japanese prison camp to guard duty at Balmoral. And he convinced me, hands down; even years later, when I was an encyclopedia salesman in Canada, I never heard a sales pitch to equal it.

"Whatever they say about this blasted bomb," he said finally, "we're going to need soldiers, if only to walk over the ruins. And we're the best there are, you know. And when the Empire goes, as it certainly will—" this was an old Colonel talking, in 1947 "—someone's going to have to leave it tidy, so that it will take the native politicians that much longer to mess it up again." He rubbed his long nose, and did his bushy-browed Aubrey Smith grin. "It'll all be done for nothing, of course, in the long run; always has been. Ask the Romans. But it's still got to be done—was that your quarter-master,

Blind Sixty, who passed the door just now? Wasn't wearing his hat—whenever that man goes about without his bonnet on, there's a crisis at hand. Someone been stealing four-by-two, probably. Anyway, young Dand, don't you ever have tea for visitors in your office? In my young day, D Company hospitality was a by-word . . ."

And when finally he had gone, he'd left me full of fine thoughts, in which I soldiered on and became Colonel of the Regiment myself, some day, maybe a general, even, with five rows of gongs, and an honourable record, and a paragraph in *Who's Who*. I tried to convince myself that he hadn't given exactly the same pep-talk to every subaltern in the battalion, but concluded that he probably had. Anyway, I applied for the appropriate signing-on forms, swithered over them, filled them in, kept them three weeks in my desk—and finally tore them up.

It wasn't just that the Colonel himself had gone by then (the new man was all right, in his precise, formal way, but not my kind of C.O., really), that the Adjutant had announced, with Bertie Woosterish cries, that he was going to take his demobilisation and make a pile in the City, bowler-hat and all, or that new subalterns were coming in and the atmosphere was changing, with the last happy-go-lucky vestiges of war-time soldiering going out and the somehow more austere sense of peace coming in. It was simply a realisation that (as Socrates and the boys no doubt said themselves) I wasn't a professional soldier.

I wondered, contemplating that broadsword on the last afternoon, how many Highland Scots really were. To fight briefly in a good cause, or for money, or for fun —these are reasons in the Highland tradition, but dedication to a lifetime of soldiering was something else.

I shoved the sword back in its scabbard, and took it across to the pipe-band office—responding, on the way, with a rude gesture to Lieutenant MacKenzie's cry of "There goes the D'Artagnan of D Company; his father was the finest swordsman in France." The pipey was perched behind his desk, looking as usual like a parrot bent on mischief; I don't remember saying goodbye to him, but I recollect that somewhere in the store-room behind him someone was singing "Macgregor's Gathering" in a nasal Gaelic tenor:

> Glenstray and Glen Lyon no longer are ours
> We're landless!—landless!—landless Gregora!

And the pipey, wagging his head, remarked:
"That's the Macgregors for ye; aye greetin' about something."

And I felt really sad, then, at the thought of leaving it all—but cheered myself up with the thought that tomorrow I'd be a free agent again, not subject to discipline or bugle-calls or King's Regulations (which was pathetic, when you think of the disciplines and calls and regulations of a civilian working life). I wouldn't have to feel responsible any more, for anyone but myself—certainly not for thirty-six hard-bitten, volatile and contrary Scotsmen who for their part could not wait to kiss the army goodbye. I would miss them, but there were definite compensations. Wee Wullie, for one, could put the entire military police force in hospital, Private Fletcher could start a Jocks' Trade Union, the whole platoon could mutiny and take to the hills, and I, the footloose civilian, could say it was nothing to do with me.

Biggest bonus of all, I could no longer be called to account for the vagaries of 14687347, Private McAuslan, J. He, henceforth, could get tight, or go absent, or set

fire to his billet, or fall in the Clyde, or assault the Lord
Provost, or lose the atomic bomb (he'd scored four out
of six on those, so far) and no one could turn a reproach-
ful eye on me. After tomorrow, he was on his own.

Tomorrow, as it turned out, was a long day. I had a
premonition that it was going to be when the truck
came to pick me up at first light to catch the morning
train out of Edinburgh; there, snuggled up by the tailboard, and looking like the last man off the beach at
Dunkirk, was the original Calamity Jock himself. By his
hideous snuffling, and the fact that he appeared to be in
the terminal stages of pneumonia, I deduced that he
had spent his last night in the Army celebrating; he was
so hung over you could have pegged him on a line. He
gave me a ghastly, red-rimmed grin as I threw my valise
over the tailboard, and croaked:

"Hullaw, rerr, sir."

"Morning, McAuslan. How are you?"

"Smashin', sir." He coughed retchingly, plucked a
mangled cigarette end from the corner of his mouth,
and wheezed: "Goad, Ah'll hiv tae give these up. Hey,
but, we're gettin' oor tickets the day, aren't we, sir?"

"That's right," I said, and beat a hasty retreat to the
front cab. I had no desire to encourage conversation
with a McAuslan who would become increasingly
garrulous as he emerged from his excesses of the night
before. There was a long train journey to the demobilisation centre at York, and while I was nominally in charge
of the party—there were four other Jocks in the back
with McAuslan—the farther I could stay away from
him the better I'd like it. If you think my non-fraternis-
ing policy deplorable, I can only reply that you haven't
seen McAuslan drying out. For that matter, you
wouldn't seek his company if he was stone-cold sober.

The truck rolled off, and I imagine we had gone all of

thirty yards before he fell over the tailboard. It transpired that he thought he had forgotten his kitbag, had risen in alarm, and toppled shrieking into the void. He was crawling out of a deep puddle like some monster emerging from Jurassic swamps, vituperating horribly, when we picked him up and bundled him into the truck again, his companions handling him gingerly.

"Tak' yer hands aff ma body!" was all the thanks they got. "Look at the state ye've got me in! Me in ma best battle-dress, too! Lookarit! Covered in glaur!"

If anything, I'd have said immersion in the puddle had cleaned it slightly; his best battle-dress, so-called, would have evoked cries of revulsion along Skid Row. He subsided in the truck, grunting and mumping and pawing the water from the greasy line of medal ribbons tacked above his left breast-pocket, from which the button was inevitably missing. As I retrieved a sodden packet of Woodbines from the puddle where he had dropped it, I had a sudden thought.

"McAuslan," I said, "have you got your travel warrant and paybooks?" One thing I didn't need was McAuslan without the documents necessary to speed him smoothly out of my life.

He suspended his toilet to rummage, breathing heavily, and produced from the recesses of his clothing two tattered lumps of paper, like very old manuscripts that have lain neglected in a damp tomb; they proved to be his Army paybooks, parts 1 and 2. But no travel warrant; he goggled dirtily when I demanded where it was, wiped his nose, and said he didnae know aboot that, but. So we had to wait, and I stamped impatiently and consulted my watch, while one of the Jocks ran back to company office, and by sheer luck returned with the warrant, which McAuslan had neglected to draw from the clerk.

"Keep it, Sempill," I told the Jock. "Don't let it, or him, out of your sight. You," I snarled at McAuslan, "sit still, or so help me I'll turn you over to the redcaps for . . . for conduct prejudicial to good order and military discipline, and you'll never get out of the Army, see?"

"Yessir. Right sir. No' kiddin', sir." The threat obviously got through to him. He was poking at the contents of his Woodbine packet; a few dripping little cylinders rapidly disintegrating into mush in his palm. "See ma bluidy fags."

"Oh, Lord," I said, "take these." And I thrust my cigarette packet into his hand, and ran to the cab. We broke the speed limit all the way up Leith walk, and arrived at Waverley Station in the nick of time to catch the train. McAuslan was last aboard, roaring in panic as he retrieved his kitbag, which had somehow slipped half-down between train and platform as we moved off. From my carriage window I saw bag and man being dragged to safety by his mates; imagine King Kong on the Empire State Building, wearing a balmoral bonnet and being enveloped in rising clouds of steam, and you have the picture.

I can't say I enjoyed that journey. Travel in British trains in the immediate post-war period was slow, uncomfortable, and involved frequent clanking halts in the middle of nowhere. It seemed inevitable that McAuslan would take it into his head to descend at one of these, and rootle under the wheels, or take off into the wilds of Berwickshire, or pull the communication cord. I stood nervously in the corridor all the way to Newcastle, being trampled and shoved and leaned on—you didn't expect to get a seat in those days—and waiting for the noises of alarm and excursion to break out farther down the train, where he and his associates were. But he was reserving his energies, apparently, for when we got over the border.

Once we reached England, he began to exhibit his best form; his hangover had presumably receded. During the halt at Newcastle he lost his bonnet in the men's lavatory and started an altercation in the refreshment room where, he alleged, they were trying to short-change him over the price of a pie and a cup of tea. (Since he could barely count beyond five, I wasn't prepared to take his word for it.) At Durham he tried to climb, smoking and coughing thunderously, into a non-smoker, whence he was ejected by an indignant dowager. He called her a cheeky auld bizzum and she threatened to complain to his commanding officer. (I was in the adjacent corridor, averting my gaze and trying to look inconspicuous.) At Darlington, where I allowed him one pint of beer at his earnest request, I was silly enough to take my eye off him, and when the guard's whistle blew he was nowhere to be seen. Fortunately the train did one of those hesitant starts, clanking a few yards and stopping, and our frantic search eventually discovered him on another platform, wrestling with one of those little football machines, all encased in glass, in which two teams of tiny metal men kick at a ball in response to little levers which you work on the outside. Beautifully ugly little Victorian creations, which seem to have vanished now. McAuslan, full of animation, was yanking the handle and roaring: "Come away the Rangairs! Itsa goal! Aw, Wullie Waddell, he's the wee boy!"

We pried him loose, ignoring his cries that he was entitled to his penny back, and just managed to get him into the guard's van.

At York, which we reached in the afternoon, we parted. The Jocks were taken off by a warrant officer,

and I went to the officers' mess, relieved in the knowledge that McAuslan would spend his last two hours in
the Army under competent military control.

"See yez at the kittin'-oot centre," said he as we went
our separate ways, and I confess to a momentary hope
that we might miss each other; for all the attachment
that had grown up between us in our chequered
acquaintance, I'd had, on the whole, just about enough.

It's one of the tricks of memory that all I can remember of my actual demobilisation is playing table billiards
in the mess while waiting for the formalities to begin;
of the process which turned me from a trusty friend of
King George into a civilian I can recall nothing, beyond
signing something, and being given a small booklet
which was my actual discharge, and informed me that I
was entitled to keep the permanent title of lieutenant,
to wear my uniform for one more month, if I wanted to,
and to consider myself a Reservist Class A. They thanked
me, politely, and told me that if I followed the signs in
the corridor I would arrive at the kitting-out centre,
where I would be issued with civilian clothes, the gift of
the Government.

It was a huge place, like an aircraft hangar, with row
upon row of counters, and suits hanging on racks, and
great square cardboard boxes. There were armies of
little men helping the newly-fledged civilians to make
their choice, and great throngs of figures in various
stages of khaki undress wandering about, rather bewildered, feeling the material as though they didn't
quite believe it was there. I remember a stout captain
in the Loyals, in his vest and service dress trousers,
doubtfully examining a civilian shirt and saying that he
didn't care for stripes, actually, and a grizzled little
corporal of Sherwood Foresters comparing a thick grey
Army issue sock in one hand, and a dark blue civilian

one in the other; his bare feet were thrust into black
civilian shoes.

I took two shirts—any shirts—and collars, and a brass
stud from the tray provided, and walked round to where
the suits were. They were mostly brown and blue, and
a long line of men in their underclothes were struggling
into trousers, and adjusting braces, and queuing up for
the long mirrors, in front of which they stood looking
rather embarrassed, turning this way and that and pat-
ting their stomachs, while the rest of us waited our
turn. The only thing in common was the close-cropped
Army hair-style; for the rest there were pale-looking
men who had spent their service in stores and offices,
and bronzed mahogany muscle-men from the Far East
and the North African garrisons—the man in front of
me, bronzed and bare to the waist, had a crude blue-
and-red tattoo on his arm, showing a knife impaling a
skull, with underneath "Death Before Disonour" (one
spelling mistake for a Hogg Market tattooist wasn't bad).
Underneath his right shoulder, when he turned, was the
white star-shape of a bullet wound, and I speculated on
whether it was the Jap 300 rifle that had done it, and
where—anywhere between Silchar Track and the Pegu
Yomas, probably. Behind me was a stout and impatient
ex-warrant officer, holding in his belly under the unaccustomed brown worsted trousers, and muttering:
"Bloody army, bloody organisation, can't even get rid
of us decently. Have you seen the quality of this rubbish? I wouldn't give it for a blanket to our dog."

The strange thing was, where you would have
expected cheerful chatter and laughter, from men who
had travelled hopefully for so long, and were now
arriving, there was very little noise at all; indeed, they
seemed quietly irritable, as though the bleak utility of
the new civilian clothing was symbolic, and they didn't

much like the look of it. Was this what civvy street was
going to be like?

On a long table to one side lay the battle-dress jackets
of those waiting to try their new suits; I wish I had a
picture of it. There were the shoulder flashes—Buffs,
Green Howards, Durhams, Ox and Bucks, Devons,
K.O.Y.L.I., North Staffords, King's Own, the yellow lion
of the Scottish Division, the shoulder flash of the
Sappers, the red and blue of the Artillery, the Welsh
black pigtail flash, and my own green and yellow strip
of tartan; the blancoed stripes and the cloth officers'
pips; the little red service chevrons, the Tate and Lyle
badge of a regimental sergeant-major; the glittering
crown and stripes of a colour-sergeant. And the ribbons
—the well-known "Spam" of 1939–45, the yellowish
rectangle of North Africa, the tricolour of France and
Germany, the green-striped ribbon of the Italian campaign, the watered colours of the Atlantic Star, and the
red-yellow-blue of Burma. And the badges in the caps—
the Britannia of the Royal Norfolks, who alone can take
a lady into barracks; the back-to-back of the Gloucesters,
the red hackle of the Black Watch, the St Andrew's
Cross of the Camerons ("two crossed bars o' quarter-
master's soap wi' auld Wimberley keekin' ower the top,"
as the pipey used to say); the Maltese Cross of the Border Regiment, the flag-carrying lamb of the Queen's, the
brown cockade of Ulster, and the white horse of
Hanover. A lot of service, a lot of time; a lot of long hot
and cold marches to battles whose echoes had died
away, and the owners, who had spent so many years
earning the little badges, were now devoting all their
minds to trouser-creases and shoulder-padding.

Most of them at least had some idea of what they
ought to look like, from their dim recollections of pre-
war days; I didn't. As I pulled up my reddish-brown

herring-bone trousers—they seemed ridiculously loose and flappy—I realised that I had never worn a formal suit in my life. At school it had been blazer and flannels, and my kilt on Sundays. I tried the waistcoat and jacket and decided I looked like a Victorian commercial travel-ler. Still, it would do; I gave way to the ex-W.O. behind me, who bustled up to the mirror and exclaimed, "God sake, more like a bleedin' kitbag with string round the middle than a bloody suit. There's room for the whole bleedin' Pioneer Corps in the crotch o' this lot."

I recovered my battle-dress jacket and kilt and went to try on a hat. They were trilbys, brown and blue, each with a tiny coloured feather peeping pathetically over the band. A stout, moustachioed Irish sergeant laid aside his rakish bonnet with its coffee-coloured plume, and placed a grey pork-pie on his cropped skull. He gulped at his reflection, and turned to me:

"Jayzus, will you look at that! The bloody silly things they expect a man to put on his head."

He must have thought exactly the same thing about his cockaded bonnet, once—but over the years he had grown into it, so to speak, his whiskers and personality had expanded with it, and now the civilian headgear looked ludicrous. He twitched it off and wandered off moodily in search of something else.

I tried on a hat; it felt and looked foolish and—what was the word?—trivial. Like the Ulsterman, I'd got used to the extravagance of military fashion. Why, in succes-sion over the years I'd worn the rakishly-tilted forage cap, the tin hat, the old solar topee, the magnificent broad-brimmed bush hat of the Fourteenth Army (which isn't just a hat, really, but a sort of portable umbrella-cum-hotel, with a razor-blade tucked into the band), the white-trimmed cap of the Indian Army cadet, the Highland tam-o'-shanter, and the red-and-white diced

glengarry with its fluttering tails. Surprising, in the austere atmosphere of a modern war. And now, this insig-
nificant thing with its tiny brim, perched foolishly above
my ears. It didn't even make me look like a gangster.

I stuffed it hurriedly into the big cardboard box I'd
been given, adding it to the pile I'd collected. Shirts,
shoes, socks, a quietish brown tie—I noticed that everyone else was doing the same thing. Nobody was going
to venture out in his civvy duds—they would wear their
uniforms at least until they got home, and gradually
transform themselves into civilians. (Remember how on
building sites, even well into the 1950s, you would see
workmen putting on old, worn battle-dress jackets after
their day's work, or faded blue R.A.F. tunics? Others,
like me, hung them away in cupboards to keep the
moths happy, and tried them on twenty years after,
puffing hopelessly as we tried to make them meet across
middle-aged spread.)

I had resumed my uniform, and was tying up my box
with string, when a voice floated over from behind a
long rack of blue suits.

"Name o' Goad," it was saying. "Hi, Mac, this a' ye've
got? Nae glamour pants? Nae long jaickets? An' no' a
pair o' two-toned shoes in the place! Ye expect me to go
oot wearin' one o' these b'iler suits?"

I should have hurried away, but the sight of Mc-
Auslan playing Beau Brummel was too good to miss. I
peeped cautiously round the end of the rack, and felt
like Cortez when with eagle eyes he gazed on the Pacific.

McAuslan was surveying himself in a mirror, striking
what he imagined to be a pose appropriate to a man
about town; either that or he was trying to keep his
trousers up with no hands. He was crouching slightly
forward, arms back, like a swimmer preparing for a
racing dive. On the back of his head was a brown pork-

pie hat, in tasteful contrast to the dark blue serge
trousers which were clinging, by surface tension, presumably, to his withers, and depending baggily to his
calves—he still had his army boots on, I noticed—and
the final flamboyant touch was provided by the identity
discs on a dirty string which he still wore over a new
civilian shirt and collar.

"Bluidy awfu'," he remarked at last, to a weary-
looking counterman. "Nae drape at a'. Youse fellas
arenae in touch. The bottom o' the breeks ought tae
hang casual-like, ower the boots. See this lot—ma feet's
just stickin' oot the end like a pair o' candles oot o' jeely-
jars."

"Who the hell d'you think you are?" said the counterman. "Ray Milland?"

"Watch it," said McAuslan warningly, and waggled
his feet to turn so that he could get a different view.
This achieved the sought-after casual break of the
trousers over the instep, inasmuch as the whole lot fell
around his ankles, and he cursed and staggered about.

"You'll pay for that lot, if you damage them!" cried
the counterman. "For God's sake, how can you try them
on without braces? Here, let's sort you out." And between them they hauled up the trousers, adjusted the
braces, and considered the result.

"Hellish," was McAuslan's verdict. "The cut's dia-
bolical. See— ma flies is doon at ma bluidy knees."

"Monsieur hasn't really got the figure, has he?" said
the counterman, a humorist in his way. "You don't
happen to have a third buttock, or something, do you?"

"None o' yer lip," said McAuslan, outraged. "Ah
didnae dae six years sojerin' just tae get pit oot in the
street lookin' like Charlie Chaplin. Fair does—could Ah
go jiggin' at the Barrowland or Green's Playhoose in the
like o' these?"

"Depends whether they go in for fancy dress," said the counterman, and McAuslan, turning in wrath, caught sight of me watching in stricken fascination. His gargoyle face lit up, and he cried:

"Hi, Mr MacNeill! Jist the man! Gie's a hand tae get sortit oot here, sir, wull ye? This fella's got nae idea."

Well, heaven knew I wasn't short of practice in rendering the subject fit for public scrutiny; after two years of "sortin' oot" McAuslan I could have valeted Gollum. I helped to adjust his trousers, approved the fit of his jacket, joined in deploring the fact that it had "nae vents up the back; they're a' the rage wi' the wide boys", and assisted in the selection of a tie. This took a good twenty minutes, while I marvelled that the man who had been notoriously the scruffiest walking wreck in the ranks of the Western Allies should be so fastidious in his choice of neckwear.

"Nae style," he sniffed, and wiped his nose. "But it'll hiv tae do till I get doon the Barras." (The Barrows is a market in down-town Glasgow where you can buy anything.) "It's no bad, but." And he pawed with grubby fingers at the muted grey tie which the counterman and I had suggested. "Whit d'ye think, sir?"

"Not bad at all," I said, and meant it. In a way, it was quite eery; there was McAuslan's dirty face, frowning earnestly from under the brim of a neat trilby, with the rest of him most respectably concealed in a blue serge suit which, considering that he was built along the lines of an orang-utan, fitted him surprisingly well. If you'd held him still, and scrubbed his face and hands hard with surgical spirit, he'd have looked quite good. Not that *Esquire* would have been bidding for his services, but he was certainly passable. I guessed that five minutes would be all he'd need to turn his new apparel into something fit for scaring birds, but just at the moment he looked more presentable than I'll swear he'd ever been in his life before.

He seemed to think so, too, for after shambling about a bit in front of the mirror, peering malevolently, he expressed himself satisfied—just.

"Ah'll tak' it," he remarked, with the resigned air of a Regency buck overcome with ennui. "But the shoulders isnae padded worth a tosser."

I'd thought he would want to stride forth in his new finery, but he insisted on packing it all into the box, and resuming his befouled and buttonless battle-dress tunic, his stained kilt, puttees, and boots, which restored him to the dishevelled and insanitary condition I knew so well.

"Nae doot aboot it, uniform's more smarter," he observed, adjusting his bonnet to the authentic coal-heaver slant over the brows. I caught sight of myself, watching him in the mirror, and was startled to see that I was smiling almost wistfully.

"Right," said he, "we're aff. Be seein' ye, china," he added to the counterman, and we made our way out into the open air, carrying our new clothes in their fine cardboard boxes. In addition I had my ashplant and a small suitcase; McAuslan humphed along with his kit-bag over his shoulder.

My train, a local to Carlisle, was due to leave in about an hour; McAuslan—after I had consulted time-tables on his behalf and checked his warrant—would have to catch a later train going through to Glasgow. I don't remember how we got to the station, but I know it was a beautiful golden August evening, and the streets were busy and the pavements crowded with people making their way home. There was time to kill, so I said to him:

"I didn't get any lunch, did you?"

"Couple o' wads'n a pie."

"Fancy a cup of tea?"

"Aye, no' hauf. Jist dae wi' a mug o' chah. Thanks very much, sir."

We made our way towards a café beside the station, and I said,

"You don't call me 'sir' any more, you know. We're civilians now."

This seemed to surprise him. He thought about it, and said:

"That's right, innit? Aye, we're oot." He shook his head. "'Magine that. It's gaunae be . . . kinda funny, innit? Bein' in civvy street. Wonder whit it's gaunae be like, eh?"

"We'll find out," I said. "Let's get in the queue." The café, short-staffed as most places were in the post-war, operated on the self-service principle, with two perspiring waitresses dispensing tea and buns at a counter. "No, hold on," I said. "You bag a table and I'll get the teas." And while McAuslan gathered up our kit, I moved quickly to the end of the queue, just getting there before a bullet-headed private in the King's Liverpool.

"Bleedin' soldiers in skirts," he muttered taking his place behind me, and as I turned to stare at him I realised I'd seen him in the demob centre earlier; sure enough, he too was carrying a cardboard box. Our eyes met, and he gave me a defiant stare.

"Awright, wack," he said truculently. "Doan't think you can throw those aboot any longer." And he indicated my pips. "Ah doan't give a —— for officers, me; niver did, see?"

There was no answer to it, now; I didn't have the Army Act behind me any longer, and any embittered ex-soldier could give me all the lip he liked. So I fell back on personality, and tried to stare him down, like a Sabatini hero quelling the canaille with a single imperious glance. It didn't work, of course; he just grinned insolently back, enjoying himself, and jeered:

"Go on, then, *leff*-tenant. What you gonna do aboot it?"

I had no idea, fortunately, or I might have done something rash. And at that moment McAuslan was at my elbow, smoothing over the incident diplomatically.

"Bugger off, scouse," he said, "or Ah'll breathe on ye."

"You'll what?" scoffed the Liverpool man, and McAuslan came in, jaw out-thrust.

"Hold it!" I said, and got between them. "Ease off, McAuslan. If our friend here wants to get cheeky with a fellow-civilian, he's entitled to. And if the fellow-civilian decides to belt the hell out of him," I went on, turning to the scouse, "that's all right, too, isn't it? You can't throw these pips at me either, son. All right?"

It startled him— it startled me, for that matter, but it worked. He muttered abuse, and I turned my back on him, and McAuslan hovered, offering, in a liberal way, to put the boot in, and gradually their discussion tailed off in dirty looks, as these things will. I collected our teas, and we got a table by the window, McAuslan still simmering indignantly.

"Pit the heid on him, nae bother," he muttered, as we sat down. "Bluidy liberty, talkin' tae you like that."

"It's a free country," I said. "Forget it."

"Aye, but—" he frowned earnestly. "Ye see whit it is; he knows you cannae peg him any longer, an' he's jist takin' advantage. That's whit he wis doin', the ——"

"Cheers," I said, smiling. "Drink your tea." McAuslan might not be a fast thinker, but when he grasped the implications of a situation he liked to explain them to feebler minds. To change the subject I asked:

"What are you going to do when you get home?"

He took an audible sip of tea and looked judicious. "Aye, weel, Ah'll tak' a look roon', see whit's daein'. Ye know. Ah'm no' hurryin' mysel'. Gaunae take it easy for a bit."

"You live with your aunt, don't you?" I remembered that the platoon roll had given "Mrs J. M. Cairns, aunt" as his next-of-kin; also, irrelevantly, that his religion was Presbyterian and his boots size 8.

"'At's right. She's got a hoose in Ronald Street. Ah don't know, but; I might get a place mysel'."

"How about a job?"

"Aye." He looked doubtful. "Ah wis on the burroo afore the war"—that is, drawing unemployment pay— "but Ah done some pipe-scrapin' up at Port Dundas, an' Ah wis wi' an asphalter for a bit. No' bad pey, but Ah didnae like workin' wi' tar. Gets in yer hair an' yer claes somethin' hellish." His face brightened. "But Ah'm no' worryin' for a bit. Ah'll tak' my time. There's this fella I know in the Garngad; Ah could get a job wi' him, if the money's right." He gave an expansive gesture which knocked over his tea-cup; with a blistering oath he pawed at it, and overturned my cup as well. In the ensuing confusion I hurriedly went for two fresh cups, leaving him apologising luridly and mopping up with his bonnet.

"Awfy sorry aboot that," he said when I returned, "makin' a mess a' ower the place. Clumsy—that's whit the R.S.M. used to say. 'Ye're handless, McAuslan.' Put the fear o' death in me, he did."

"Well, he won't do that any more," I said.

"Naw. That's right." He took a gulp of tea, and sighed. "He was a good man, but, that Mackintosh. He was gae decent tae me." And he looked across at me. "So wis you. So wis Sarn't Telfer, an' Captain Bennet-Bruce..."

"This is worse than Naafi tea, isn't it?" I said, and he agreed, remarking that he could have produced better himself, through the digestive process. Then suddenly he asked,

"Whit ye gaunae do in civvy street yersel', sir?"

"Newspapers," I said. "I'm going to be a reporter."

"Zattafact?" He beamed. "Here, that'll be rerr. Goin' tae the fitba' matches—free?"

"Probably."

"An' —an', interviewin' fillum stars?" he went on, his imagination taking wing.

"Well, I shouldn't think—"

"—an' gettin' the goods on the bad bastards in the corporation, like Alan Ladd in the pictures! Here, that's a gran' joab! Ah could jist be daein' wi' that." You could see him envisaging himself perched on the corner of an editor's desk, with his hat tilted back, addressing Veronica Lake as "baby".

"Aye, but," he added, and fell silent, and I knew what he was thinking. He had come into the Army illiterate, and in spite of the Education Sergeant's perseverance, he was going out not much better. He frowned at his cup. "Ah doubt Ah wouldnae be up tae it, though." He drank again. "Ah'll jist see whit's daein'."

I looked across at him, scruffy and hunched over his cup, and had a sudden picture of thirty years on, and saw him as one of these seedy wee Glasgow men one encounters coming out of pubs—the threadbare coat, the dirty white scarf knotted to conceal the absence of collar (and sometimes of shirt), the broken shoes, the thin greying hair defiantly brushed, and still with a gamin jauntiness in the way they shuffle along, looking this way and that with their bright, beaten eyes. And I had a thought that choked me—of the heat and dust and thunder of Alamein, and the flower of the finest

military machine ever to come out of the Continent
being broken and scattered, and chased out of Africa,
and I felt a terrible anger at—at I don't know what. The
world, or the system, or something. My hand was shaking, I know, as I put down my cup.

It subsided after a moment or two, while I carefully
drank my tea, into an uncomfortable feeling that was
half annoyance and half embarrassment. I can't define
it, even now. I suppose it sprang from all I knew about
McAuslan, and all the trouble and alarm and impatience
and fury he had caused me, and the responsibility I'd
carried for him. But in the past I'd always known what
to do about it; we had been bound rigidly inside the
Army framework. Now that was all over, but the feelings were still there, without the means to cope with
them—or with him. I was worried about him—God
knew he hadn't been fit, most of the time, to go about
unattended in uniform; what he would be like in civilian
life, with no one to watch him, and berate and bully
him and pick up the can for him, I couldn't imagine.
Strictly speaking, it was none of my business; it was
almost impertinent to think that it was. But responsibility doesn't just end—or if it does, the feeling of it
doesn't.

"Here," I said, "I'll have to shift myself if I'm to
catch that train." I shoved a threepenny bit under my
cup and started to collect my things, knowing that I
couldn't just go off and leave it as it was. Without really
thinking, while we both got up and made the prelimin-
ary noises of farewell, I pulled out my pen and a scrap
of paper, and scribbled my home address. It was just a
gesture; I had no connections, I couldn't offer any con-
structive help, and I knew it. But it seemed the least I
could do.

"That's my home, and phone number," I said, with a

momentary qualm at the thought of what McAuslan might do to the internal economy of the G.P.O. if he tried to make a telephone call. "If there's anything I can do . . . you know, any time, if you think I can help, or . . . I mean, you need any . . . I mean, have any problems . . ." I was making a right hash of it, I realised. "Anyway, that's where I am."

"Oh, ta," he said. "Very nice of ye." And he took the paper, handling it reverently, as he always did when confronted with the mysteries. But there was an odd expression on his rumpled face as he looked at it, a trace of that slow, dawning self-assertion that I remembered before his court martial, a slight tilt of his head as he looked at me, a stiffening of the Palaeolithic frame.

"Thanks very much," he said. "But yez don't need tae worry aboot me. Not at a'. Ah'll be fine; nae bother." It wasn't anything like a snub, just a self-respecting reminder of what I'd said myself earlier; that we were both civilians now. I could have kicked myself for my clumsiness, and tried to shrug off my embarrassment.

"You know," I said, "it would be nice to . . . to keep in touch."

God, I thought, what am I saying? Keep in touch with McAuslan; the mind boggled.

"Och, sure," he said, jauntily. "We'll be around."

We were outside the café by this time; the station entrance was just along the way.

"Well," I said, and held out my hand. "Good luck, McAuslan." And why I added it, I don't know, but I said: "Thanks for everything." It was not a statement that could be defended on any logical ground, but I meant it.

"Och," he said, "s'been nice knowin' ye. Orrabest, sir."

We shook, and picked up our parcels.

"Aye, weel," he said, "Ah'll jist tak' a dauner roon the toon afore my train goes."

"Mind you don't miss it."

"Nae fears," he said, and with a nod set off down the pavement towards a pedestrian crossing, cardboard box in one hand, kit-bag on the other shoulder—baunchling jauntily along, with one hose-top already wrinkling down to his ankle, his scruffy kilt swinging. I watched him go, slightly sad, but—I must confess it honestly—with considerable relief. I knew he wouldn't get in touch—even if he wanted to, the mechanics of the thing would defeat him. I just hoped the world would be kind to him, the sturdy, handless misfit, with his bonnet cocked at a pathetically jaunty angle, and the other hose-top now descending to join the first.

He turned on to the crossing, and I moved off to the station entrance, and just as I reached it there was a hideous shriek of brakes from behind me, a woman screamed in alarm, someone shouted, and I looked round to see a lorry half-slewed round on the crossing, and under its near front wheel a cardboard box, squashed flat. For an instant my heart died, and then to my relief I saw him, skipping like a startled sloth from under the very bonnet, his kit-bag falling to the pavement, where its top burst, scattering the contents among the pedestrians.

There were oaths and cries, mainly from McAuslan, standing raging in the gutter, while a red-faced driver leaned from the lorry's cab, hurling abuse at him. Phrases like "bloody daft jay-walker, where the 'ell d'you think you're goin'?" and "You in yer bluidy van, ye near kilt me!" floated on the summer evening air. Then the driver was descending from his cab, McAuslan was stooping to gather the gruesome litter that had

fallen from his bag, and at the same time was directing
a flood of colourful invective over his shoulder.

"Ah wis oan the crossin', ye daft midden!"

"Nowhere bloody near it! Niver even looked! Just
come slap across t'road!"

"Away, you, an' bile yer can!"

"Think you own t'bloody street, then?"

On the pavements, people had stopped. So had the
traffic, with the lorry blocking one side of the road, and
horns were honking. A small crowd was gathering, as
McAuslan, still exchanging personalities with the driver,
scooped up his effects and stuffed them into his bag. A
policeman was approaching—no, there were two policemen, and a bus conductor, who by his gestures appeared
to be prepared to offer evidence.

I watched, fascinated. My first instinct was to go to
the scene of the upheaval, naturally, but then I checked.
No one was hurt, there was nothing to it; the disorderly
idiot had just managed to put his foot in it again, and
there was no useful purpose to be served by interfering.
I watched the gendarmes arrive with official calm, while
the lorry driver, full of virtuous outrage, stated his case,
and McAuslan, protesting vehemently, pointed to the
squashed ruins of the box beneath the wheel.

"Ma new suit! Ma new civvy shoes! Look at yon! Hoo
the hell am Ah gaunae be able to wear them noo? Him
an' his bluidy van . . ." With his bonnet gone, his hose-
tops down, his face contorted with misery and rage, and
his tunic and kilt looking as though they were joining in
the general depression, he was a woeful sight to see.
"Ah'm no' hivin' this! Yon man's a road-hog! He near
did for me, so he did!"

One of the policemen was ushering him back across
the pavement; the other was directing the driver to get
his van in to the side. One of the small throng watching

stepped forward and picked up McAuslan's kit-bag, unfortunately by the wrong end, and the contents came cascading out again. And I froze as I saw, among the litter of unwashed laundry and oil-smeared clothing, the unmistakable brassy glitter of rounds of .303 ammunition, tinkling away across the pavement.

"Oh, no!" I exclaimed aloud, as the second policeman stooped and picked up one of the rounds in one hand—and the old sword bayonet in the other—looked at them, and then at McAuslan, and then drew himself up purposefully.

I didn't waste time wondering how he'd got live ammunition in his luggage; souvenirs, maybe—he was idiot enough. It wouldn't have surprised me if that kit-bag had also contained several live grenades and a two-inch mortar. Sufficient that he had got himself into dire trouble, and the Law were taking out their notebooks, while the protesting author of the scene was backed against the wall, roaring:

"Keep the heid! Whit aboot yon lorry-driver then? Ah'm no' hivin' it! The man's a menace. . ."

The lorry-driver had come back to watch, and doubtless contribute his quota, the small crowd were looking on astonished, amused, intrigued. The second policeman was holding out a handful of live rounds, speaking sternly, and the ape-like, hounded wretch in the middle was protesting violently and obviously wishing he could burrow under the wall.

I had taken a half-pace forward, and stopped. What did I think I was going to do, anyway? Conditioned by years of sorting things out for McAuslan, standing between him and authority, taking responsibility for him, I had been about to intervene. And then the wonderful realisation flashed across my mind. It wasn't my place to, any longer. Three hours ago it would have been my bounden duty—and now? Legally speaking, I was no longer responsible for McAuslan's random wanderings in front of lorries, for his offering insulting language, for his being illegally in possession of Army property, to wit, live ammunition, or for his resistance to arrest which would probably follow. I had no longer any right to interfere. He was his own man, now, and it would be sheer patronising officiousness to pretend otherwise. I was (as his own attitude had reminded me) a mere civilian, with no authority over him. "It's nothing to do with me," I actually said aloud, and a passer-by looked curiously at me. And dammit, while I might feel a sentimental concern for him, responsibility was something else. Besides, I knew from bitter experience what getting involved with McAuslan was like; there was no future in it. He was free, white (well, greyish) and twenty-one, let him fight his own battles for a change, and—and I had a train to catch in three minutes.

So I swore, and shook my head for the thousandth time, turned to a military policeman in the station entrance and said: "Would you mind keeping an eye on my things for a moment, corporal?" And then I pulled down my bonnet, took a firm grip on my ashplant, said "Oh, hell" with deep weariness, and like a man re-shouldering an enormous burden, but with a strange lightness of heart, strode off purposefully towards the group on the other side of the road.

A NOTE ON THE TYPE

This book was set in Caledonia, a Linotype face designed
by W. A. Dwiggins. It belongs to the family of printing
types called "modern face" by printers—a term used to
mark the change in style of type letters that occurred about
1800. Caledonia borders on the general design of Scotch
Modern, but is more freely drawn than that letter.

This book was printed and bound by
The Book Press, Inc., Brattelboro, Vermont.

Binding design by Susan Mitchell.